BURNOUT *Baby*

A STREET-RACING EROTICA NOVELLA BY V. RIVIÈRE

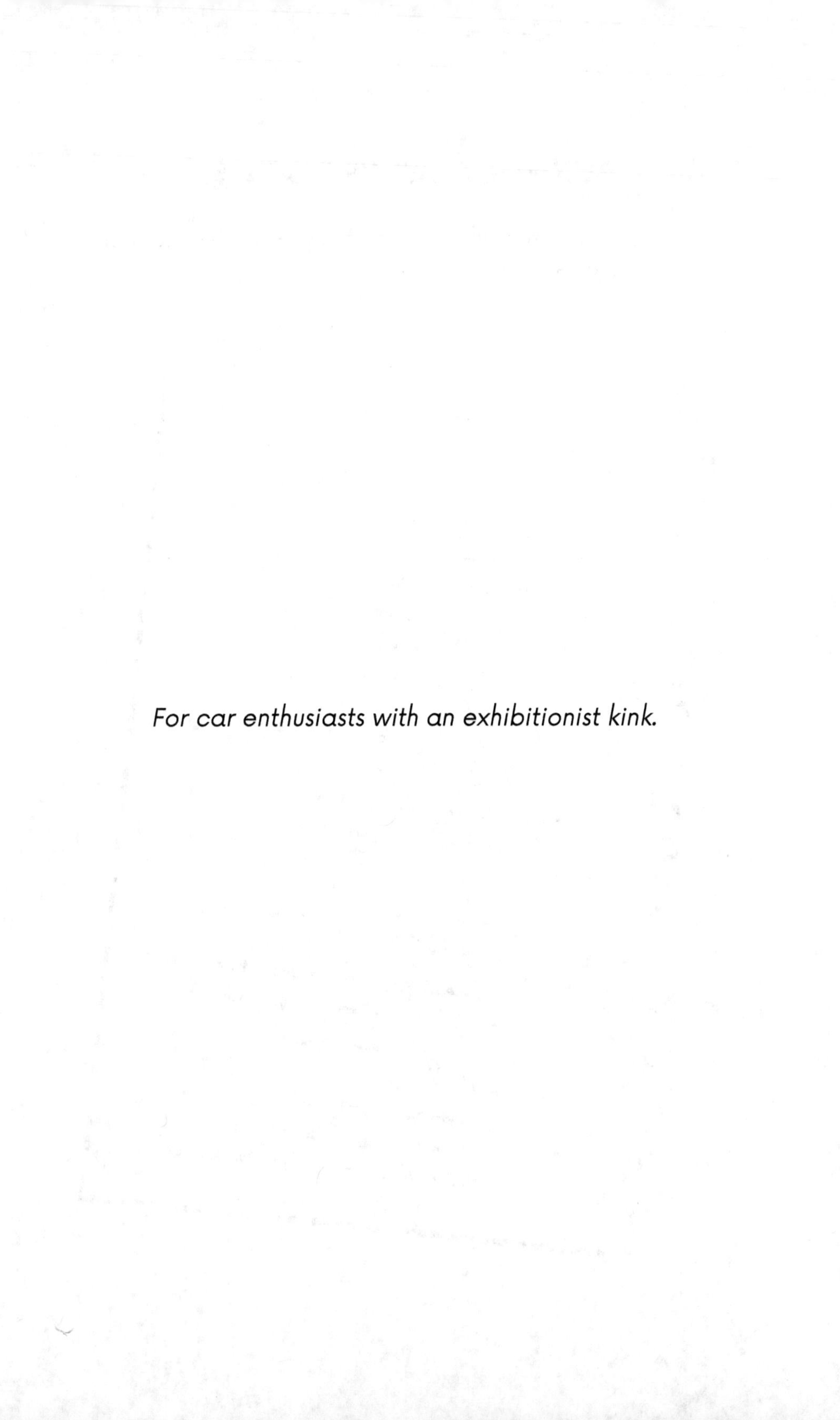

For car enthusiasts with an exhibitionist kink.

BURNOUT BABY'S PLAYLIST

Listen to the full playlist on my YouTube channel (www.youtube.com/@v.riviere)!

memory reboot — Narvent and VØJ
after life — Lowx
next to you — Øneheart
hospital — Dollcore
fainted — Narvent
with you — Altare
on the verge — Teenwxve
you're not there — Offl1nk
let it burn — Spyral and Mitrowave
fictional world — Les
drowning in my memories — MrNotYet
drowning — Vowl and Antent
lost lately — Inan
if i could see you for a second i know i wouldn't blink — New Friends
snowfall — Øneheart and Reidenshi
stellar — Siedlonely and Énouement
hope to see you again — Antent
shattered dreams — Sapphyre
memories — Leadwave
mist — Entris and Shibíre
interstellar — Pandora, Chillwithme and cødy

AUTHOR'S NOTE

The story you are about to read is a spin-off from the main series *The Apocalys Empire*. You don't need to have read the other books to understand this one, as it's just for entertainment and not an essential addition to the main plot, but you might come across a few terms or mentions of characters that you'll fail to understand.

Please see the '*Other Books by the Author*' section at the end of the novella for all the info you need on my main work!

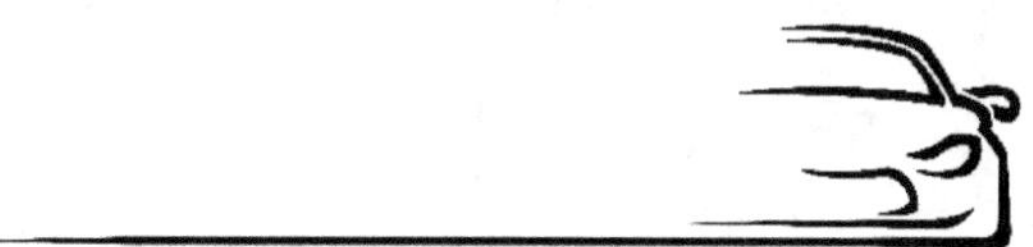

CONTENT WARNING

Bad language, explicit sexual scenes, morally reprehensible actions, illegal actions, suggestive illustrations.

TABLE OF CONTENTS

whatever it is, I'm available

PROLOGUE

In the City of Ursley, 5 Months Ago.

My legs shake with anticipation, a nervous energy coursing through me. No matter how many times I wipe my hands on my jeans, they stay clammy and warm. My heart beats in sync with the steady drip of oil from the container across the room. I glance around and spot a weird clock made from a used tire on the wall—it's eleven p.m. Luckily, the customers won't start requesting rides for a few hours, giving them time to get thoroughly drunk, some to the point of passing out.

In these moments, I'm reminded of how much I've changed. A couple of years ago, I was still in college. Now, I can barely afford an apartment in the poorest district of Greensburg. Life has a way of telling everyone nothing is forever. And by leading me back to my former campus in Ursley, it makes me realize that no matter how much I've accomplished since then, it's not enough to escape my past. It doesn't matter how resourceful I am when shame and regret can still take over my every thought.

"Jade, come in," War's gruff voice calls from inside his office. It's only by chance that our paths crossed. Normally, I wouldn't even dare look up in his presence. This man has a certain reputation. They call him *'The King of the Streets'*. Apparently, he was once linked to a mafia in Greensburg, though no one knows much about it. War is highly attuned to the rumors circulating and often uses them to his advantage while keeping his secrets. But even a meticulously managed rumor can go wrong.

One of those whispers about a year ago led me to him. He needed a driver to collect information about a wedding in the city where I was born and offered a lot of money for someone to pass by, snap pictures, and leave.

I was *that* driver.

The job got me more money than bringing party-goers home from the clubs at night ever could. In just one evening, I made triple what I would legally earn in a week. Since then, I've been practically begging to help War with anything else he might need me for.

Standing up, I empty my lungs from the air to relax my tense muscles. Dealing with him isn't a new thing for me, but his hostile attitude has always triggered my fight-or-flight response.

The garage War chose for his office is nothing but a façade, a legit business hiding his real intentions.

Out of the corner of my eyes, I see the mechanics working on a fancy truck—one you'd typically find featured on the cover of magazines intended for the wealthy people. The campus has a lot of these loaded kids. The ones we envy and gossip about. Frost's prized generation, the ultimate *goal* for most—Frost's shining diamonds. A city far better than any capital of the world. It's like the glory of Hollywood, the wealth of Vegas, and the sophistication of Paris all in one. A big, bright target that ordinary people can only dream of.

For us, driving on Frost's strip—where all the luxury boutiques and expensive restaurants are—feels wrong in some way. Over there, cars cost as much as the building I live in. It's total madness to be around such fortune.

I raise my hand to knock on the door, but it suddenly jerks open. My eyes widen as they rest on the imposing man in front of me. Arms and thighs as thick as my duffel bag, a dark look on his face, and a height rivaling a basketball player. I Immediately lower my chin. "Sorry," I mutter quietly.

"What are you doing?" he asks, his voice both commanding and insulting.

I inspect his shiny black boots, tracing with my gaze the leather trapping the hem of his cargo pants. "I heard rumors," I begin, my voice barely above a whisper, worried he might think my presence is an insult. My gaze lingers on the single finger motioning for me to lift my eyes. I comply, drawn not to his intense stare but to the deep frown on his forehead.

"So you said in your text." He lets go of the handle and turns to walk inside the office. Leaving the door open, I take it as an invitation to enter.

"Whatever it is, I'm available," I say with conviction. Trying to show I need the money without sounding desperate, I straighten up and raise my chin.

He hums thoughtfully. "It's *different* from what you've done in the past, kid," War warns, chuckling as if doubting my skills. He shouldn't, because everyone is aware he's the first to know when something happens on the street. I have participated in many street races in the past, and even if I don't always win them, I know how to drive. I know what it takes to be *good* at it.

"My car is yours," I assert, emphasizing my statement with a nod as he settles behind his imposing wooden desk, cluttered with documents. My eyes scan the space—guns, money, phones... It's like each object mocks the path I find myself drawn into. I hate myself for it. Crime for money, because a normal job doesn't pay enough with Greensburg's living costs becoming like Frost's.

A raised eyebrow appears out of his permanent scowl, an obvious sign showing that men like him are not to be messed with, spoken to with a nasty tone and disrespected. "You worked for me in the past, and you did a great job. But this time, someone from Frost asks me to find her capable *men*," he reveals, pretending to be apologetic.

It's an insult he thinks I can't compete for the job because I'm a woman. "You know how I drive. I can do everything a man can do," I exclaim passionately, anger rising. "If not *better*." I bite my lip to hide the pleading tone that won't help my case trying to convince him.

He rests his elbow on the desk and props his chin on his fingers, giving me a pitying look. "Tell me Jade, can you kill someone if I ask you to?" he questions suddenly.

My eyes find the guns again. "What?" I lock my knees in place to hide my uneasiness.

"It's not just driving this time. You'll have to be ready for anything, including carrying heavy boxes." His patronizing tone is infuriating, more so than being denied. It's humiliating.

"I can carry *boxes*," I declare, crossing my arms. Working with War has always been rewarding. He's the boss everyone wants, willing to get his hands dirty if necessary, and fall with his troops if they're loyal. I don't feel useless when I'm with him. He always has a little comment to reassure me or a silly task if motivation is lacking. Just like in the army.

Without subtlety, his gaze travels the length of my body, stopping on my arms, and a gleam dances in his eyes. "Don't take it personally, but the types of boxes we're talking about are a lot heavier than cereals." *Asshole.* "I've got your profile for future jobs, but forget about this one."

I'm about to embarrass myself more, ready to sacrifice my dignity. "I—" I begin, but my words are abruptly cut by the ringing of a phone somewhere in the chaotic mess of his desk.

"I'll call you," War says dismissively, not wanting to hear my pleading.

I drop my arms and swallow back insults. If the contractor comes from Frost, the job is going to be paid in literal gold. *Gold* I'll never see.

Head lowered, feeling frustrated and resigned, I walk out of the office without a word. As I drag my feet out of the garage, kicking the pebbles I see on the ground, a laugh travels to my ears. Raising my head, I notice one of War's mechanics. He's taking a drag from a cigarette while seated on a neglected car bench outside. With his legs spread wide, a mischievous look on his face, and his fingers caressing the bit of skin protruding from the hole in his pants, I come to a complete stop. His medium-length black hair is brushed back, and I notice ink covering every inch of his flesh. Even his face is no exception.

He chuckles again, showing his teeth, but bites his lower lip when he sees my confused look. I glance down, thinking I wore something wrong.

"Every time I see someone coming out of War's office, they either look very happy or very depressed. Just like you. It's one or the other," he notes, amused, with a smirk I can only read as condescending.

My body turns fully toward him. "I'm not looking depressed. You're exaggerating." I roll my eyes as he inhales the smoke. His head drops against the headrest as he exhales, briefly hiding his face in the white cloud. But his almond-shaped eyes capture mine almost instantly. "Every time I see a mechanic, they're either smoking or drinking. It's one or the other," I add, matching his mocking tone.

He grins and shifts to the right to leave a free seat next to him. Patting the empty space, he invites me to join. "That's because being a mechanic is fucking depressing."

I check my phone for the time, but not seeing any notification from my app, I put it in my back pocket and walk toward the guy. My involvement in the illegal street racing world has made me naturally cautious about my surroundings and the people I meet. Being out at night with a man I don't know has me hesitating, but seeing the look in his eyes and the lack of muscles in his arms is enough for me to get close. He doesn't raise any alarms and if he ever tries anything, War's not far. The boss might be a criminal, but if the rumors are to be trusted, he's not the kind to torture innocent people—that would be the *beast* everyone talks about in Ursley.

Avoiding his gaze, I can feel him studying my profile, his penetrating stare making me tense. It's been ages since I've had a guy's attention, and it's easily forgettable. "Are you sure it's not working for War?" I ask, giggling nervously. Unsure of what to do with myself, I squeeze my hands between my thighs, and try to avoid any contact with his knees. He retrieves his pack of cigarettes from his pocket and extends it to me, a silent offer I decline with a shake of my head.

"No, the boss is fine. Pay is good and we can use the clients' cars when we want to get out for a bit," the mechanic explains, trying his best to not suffocate me by blowing behind us. "You're here for one of his jobs?"

I snort at my own thoughts—*why else would I be here?* "Yeah—well. It didn't work out." My shoulders shrug, aiming to appear unbothered about the bitter rejection.

"Explains the look," he mumbles to himself with a breathy chuckle. As he closes his eyes, I spot the black tattoos on his eyelids, two spots I can't quite make out. "Heard a bit about it. Client is from Frost, apparently." His voice is muffled by of the smoke he insists on keeping in his mouth a little longer.

"Do you work for War? I mean, the *jobs*." Given the questionable nature of what he offers, I have to be careful who I talk to. Still, it dawns on me someone employed here might have some insight into the sort of work War does outside his garage business.

"I find him cars when he needs them, and recommend some friends, but other than that, being at the garage is enough for me," he states, not blinking once. I'm not sure if he tries to give me sweet eyes, or if he is really good at not blinking. "You?"

"I worked for him in the past," I admit with a nod. "I'm a driver," I reveal while pointing at my chest, feeling some shyness creeping in. Some people have mocked me because of it. They've scoffed at my appearance, claiming I don't have *the look*—whatever it means. Yet ironically, it was the only skill I had that I could use after the trial.

"A driver," he repeats, impressed. "Must be at the top of his list."

I grimace, frustration evident as my nose scrunches in annoyance. If anything, I usually have to plead for any scraps the others don't want. "Not really," I reply tersely. My phone chimes in my back pocket, the first of many notifications I'll have throughout the night. Drunk people are ready to go home, and by the time I'm back in Greensburg, I'm sure most of my clients would have already gone into one of my competitors' cars. And since I missed out on the opportunity with War, I'm not letting any chance to make money slip through my fingers tonight.

You have received a request for a ride, swipe to find out more, it says.

"I'll have to go," I announce as I stand up and accept the demand. If I drive over the legal limit and commit a few infractions along the way, I might get to the Business City before two in the morning. "Sorry. It was nice to meet you," I send distractedly over my shoulder, as I rush toward my 240SX with its mismatched red, white, and black panels.

"What's your—" he shouts from the bench, but I quickly slam the door shut and bring the engine back to life. At first, I tried to only accept rides during the day, but I quickly realized I hated traffic and the city when it's awake. There's a special emotion when you drive at night. The darkness feels so peaceful when only the headlights of my car illuminate the streets. Greensburg almost feels like a décor from a retro movie. Maybe it's the only thing that keeps me going.

a ghost from the past

CHAPTER 1

In the City of Greensburg, Present.

I don't feel too great, but I deserve it. The guilt always hits me like a punch to the gut. Yet, it's what I have to endure because it's all my fault. It's who I am now, a *murderer*. And I don't deserve peace—I deserve the hatred. My family cut me out of their lives, my friends turned their backs on me, and all these people I've hurt are right to blame me. The consequences were tough, and they still are, but this is what I have to do: face my fears and deal with it all. I owe it to the memory of the girl I killed. And today is the anniversary of her death.

It's no coincidence I'm at the cemetery so early. I've learned to make myself invisible as the date gets closer. Doing my best not to cross paths with any of her relatives. I respect their privacy but also want them to know, after all these years, I'm still deeply sorry. While I may never be forgiven, and no words can bring their daughter back to life, I keep going and won't let guilt stop me from placing flowers on her grave.

Three years ago, I was a totally different person. People knew me as the girl who always partied, the one they'd call first when they wanted to have fun. Going to college with my friends is a memory I still think about. It was more about having a good time than studying. It's true we spent most of our days in abandoned locations and frat houses, than being in classrooms. But with the partying came alcohol, drugs, and sex.

Unlike my friends, who didn't care much about cars, I couldn't separate myself from mine. Alcohol and driving don't mix —a lesson I've learned the hard way because I was *stupid*. Because I was a moron, an idiot without a brain. Because impressing my friends with my skills was more important than the life of a human being.

I've been sober ever since. Not only because I risk jail if I'm caught with even a little alcohol in my blood, but also because I'm terrified of losing control again. After the accident, I couldn't even use hand sanitizer, fearing the smell might somehow mess with my senses again. It was a mess; I was at my lowest.

Kneeling on the square of cloth carefully laid out in front of the dark-gray marble tomb, I place a bouquet of white chrysanthemums right next to engraved plaques and nearly empty candleholders.

Seeing her photo in front of my eyes feels like being stabbed in the heart. Abigail was my age when I ended her life. The what-ifs, the possibilities, are what I have a hard time dealing with. Three years, yet the remorse doesn't lessen. I'm trying to live with it—the new *me*. But it's a work in progress.

Softly laying my hand flat on the stone, I breathe out, "I'm sorry." Opening them again, I reach for my bag and take out two new candles I bought at the gas station on my way here. Setting them in front of me, I take out my matches and light them. The little dancing flames, fighting against the wind, are beautiful. The wind, like the warmth, can disappear at any moment. It's a stark reminder that only time is permanent. Peace can also be lasting, if only we allow it to be.

The leaves dropping from their branches attract my attention, and I finally get back on my feet. The morning air is refreshing and helps with my racing thoughts. I'm worried about the future, about what I'll become tomorrow, but the present is all that matters.

I shake off the dirt from my jeans and say my goodbyes—a simple nod and a look at her pristine memorial.

As I stroll along the cemetery path, I read the engravings and notice the fading flowers. All these people have loved ones, no matter how long they've been gone. They all have people who care about them. It weighs on me, and I hope to have a well-tended grave someday. By then, will my family and I be talking? Will I have friends again? No one wishes for a lonely life, but for some, it's inevitable.

Lost in my head again in the parking lot, I know I've spent too much time here as I see a familiar minivan pull up. Unsurprisingly, anxiety makes my heart beat faster and I immediately lower my head to rush to my car at the far end. In one swift motion, I'm behind the wheel, fastening my seatbelt, and turning on the engine.

I wish I was invisible when I exit. I wish my gaze didn't meet that of Abigail's mother. The years have softened her attitude toward me a bit, even if the loathing persists. And I know my bouquet and candles will end up in the trash.

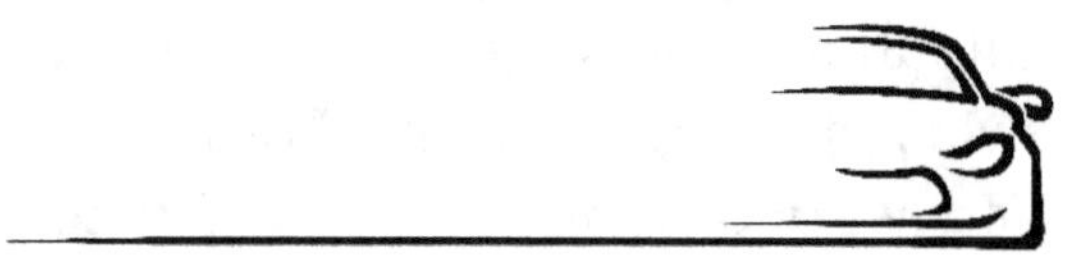

I drive through Greensburg, music playing in the background, as I try not to get too frustrated by the mass of tourists crowding the streets for the city's centennial. While I do my best to ignore it all, I'm desperately waiting for the sun to go down already. Maybe I'll check in with the group I usually race against in Greensburg. Lately, street races have been less frequent. Rumor has it, the wealthy residents of Frost are trying to take over the area, and most of the drivers have stopped waiting for the organizers to fight back.

It could also be the crime rate hitting an all-time high in the Business City. Everyone's scared of what the mafias might do. Some say War's been recruiting for permanent spots on his team, but sadly I can't confirm that. I'd be the first to jump at a chance for steady income, even if it means abandoning my morals and everything my dad, a law-abiding detective, taught me.

Even though it's not my usual thing, I've listed my profile for the day. With my near-perfect rating, customers book my car quickly. I'm eagerly accepting them as they come. My rent is due in some days, and my bank account severely needs a couple more digits for my sanity. I always manage to survive the month somehow. Working every day relentlessly has its perks. It isn't like I'm sacrificing much besides some rest.

The phone mounted on my windshield lights up with a notification. A message that makes me check the contact twice, not expecting it. War's got something for me—*finally*—and wants me to call him soon or he'll offer the gig to someone else. It doesn't take much more for me to veer my 240SX to the side of the road downtown, putting it in neutral.

For the past twenty days, I've been walking the line between persistence and harassment. Sending him texts, anxiously waiting anything he might need me for. My limbs had grown restless, itching for something more than just to be a chauffeur. It's very easy to get addicted to the danger of doing something forbidden. I think it's human nature to always look out for the rush and the adrenaline. The black market, the illegal, gives plenty of opportunities for that. But what has me hooked is the paycheck that comes with doing a good job.

I don't let my brain process his message that I suddenly open his contact with shaky fingers. The ringing worsens my nerves, so I bite my nails, hoping my heart will calm down.

"Jade," he greets monotonously, no doubt expecting me. I'm not proud of my pestering, but desperate times call for desperate measures.

My dignity be damned, I have no shame and don't plan on apologizing for it. "I'm available," I immediately blurt. In response, I hear his mocking laughter, but War's used to my antics by now. He knows that even if I'm not loyal to him, I am to money. And money he has, which makes *him* the one I need to keep happy.

"I know, kid. You're also goddamn irritating." He sighs, sounding a bit exhausted. "I need to check someone's business. Since you're already in Greensburg and the target is close by, I figured you'll be up for the job," he states, well aware I wouldn't decline even if the job was on the other side of the country.

Nodding energetically, I quickly ask, "Who? Where?" Already mentally rearranging my schedule for the next couple of days.

"You drive by, observe, and give me the lowdown on exactly *who* you see," he explains, emphasizing every word as if it's a complex task. "And Jade, I want you to be a *ghost*."

"Of course," I reply, ditching the nail-biting long ago to nervously nibble at the skin of my fingers.

"Two hundred. Good for you?" he asks, fully aware I'm not one to haggle over payment.

"Great. Who's the target?" A car behind me honks in annoyance as I'm parked awkwardly on the sidewalk. Ignoring the irritation, I try to blend into my seat. If I'm invisible, there are no problems anymore.

"Maddox Ryder," he reveals. At the mention of this name, my skin tightens and my hairs bristle, an uncontrollable reaction. The farther people are from this monster, the *better*. He's like a legend, a story that should never be told at the risk of signing someone's death sentence. This man should be locked up for good—in a facility reserved for the worst of humanity. A hole in the world where we could forget about them. Whenever the *mob* is mentioned in the city, the name *Madd Ryder* is always linked to it. I've even heard people say he's a cannibal for God's sake—what a disgusting human being.

But money calls, so I answer. "He has a club: the Balkans. It's just a few blocks from the cabaret. You can't miss it, black venture and a double-headed eagle on the doors. I need you to tell me if he's with someone other than his men. He might be working with competition. I need to know that," War declares, his tone grave.

"I don't know his competition," I confess apologetically. None of the tasks I've been given so far have relied on me knowing their connections and contacts. As War told me in the past, what made my profile interesting to him was my ignorance of the people ruling over the underworld in Greensburg. Though, I suspect it's a choice on his part to keep me in the dark. If I don't know anything, I can't spread rumors and tell others what I've seen.

"It's fine. Forget about it. You go there, see if you can spot anything. You come to me tonight for your report, got it?"

"Understood." Immediately, I hang up, disable ride requests from the app, and direct the car toward the Balkans club. Ready to welcome that feeling that comes when you do something wrong.

new players in Greensburg

CHAPTER 2

In Greensburg.

I parked on a nearby street, not to hide my car, but because the roads are blocked today. They're packed with people, making it impossible to drive. As a result, the cars are lined up bumper to bumper, like bodies packed into a crowd. I can't spot the Balkans from this distance, let alone take any photos. But with so many individuals around, it's easier to blend in.

And, I take advantage of it by pretending to take pictures with my phone as a passerby might do. It doesn't take long before I'm standing directly in front of this double-headed eagle. Seeing this emblem alone makes me think of all the ways this could go wrong. I've never been this close to guys like *them,* dangerous. Someone might spot me, or worse—remember my face.

The idea has me scanning my surroundings, my eyes darting in every direction to catch any cameras. I spot them on the tiny balconies, pointed at the street and entrance, watching over the buildings. All of this makes me bite my lips nervously and lower my head, but now I worry I draw even more attention to myself—having stupidly stared at every lens in the area.

Instead of overthinking it, I straighten my shoulders and smooth down the fabric of my black dress. I know my fishnet stockings don't fit in, I pretend to look for someone while watching people come and go from the club. None of them seem to give off any criminal vibes, maybe on purpose. Eventually, I walk inside showing as much confidence as I can. Pretending to be someone I'm not.

The ambiance of a nightclub during the day is unique, but this one seems to adapt perfectly. The bar is in full swing, the lighting is a mix of subtle and vibrant, people dance, some sip drinks while others prefer to talk and look around. The atmosphere here is alive, *excited.*

Slowly, I make my way toward the waiter behind the counter and choose a place where I can see the doors, the room, and the staircase at the back. From here, I can even take out my phone without being noticed.

This job might be easier than I thought.

My gallery quickly fills up with random faces as I drink a soda. The straw between my lips, I freeze when two people walk in: a man and a woman. Both of them have this aura I can only describe as *threatening*. They might be the ones War was referring to, the ones who might be involved with Maddox Ryder's business.

Without realizing it, I catch myself with my mouth wide open, ogling at the woman as her siren eyes sweep across the room. Wearing a tight black dress that fits her like a glove and high stilettos looking like weapons, she reminds me of the models you see on jewelry ads. The way she walks attract the attention of the people around, causing some to even stop their discussions just to watch her. They hold their breaths as she decides if this place is good enough for her. When I point my phone to take a picture, I'm in awe. She feeds on the stares, rolls her hips, plays with her hair, while the man sends glares into the eyes of all others in the room. They might be together, but the way he tries to keep his distance from her and the commanding glower she gives him is enough to suggest *she* might be his *boss*.

I've never met a mob boss before—other than Maddox—and it feels unreal, like a movie. But I can't see her as anything else.

The man by her side takes the lead, and together they climb the stairs. As they disappear from the nightclub's main floor, the energy picks up again, and people resume what they were doing. I'm left staring at the empty space where they stood just a second ago, unsure of exactly what I'm supposed to do next. However, my phone's screen turning off on itself between my hands brings me back to reality. The last thing I want is to run into Maddox, especially since I'm not sure that the last time I took his picture at his wedding, he saw me. It was a long time ago, but when people like them have enemies on all fronts, I can imagine files upon files of information stored somewhere safe.

I fish out my wallet in a haste to throw money for my soda. In an instant, I'm up on my feet, chin lowered, fleeting the place before the people have time to register anything, I'm gone. I make my way through the crowded space, elbowing some people, and try to stay calm. Practically running to my car, I call War, wanting to bail on the mission altogether.

What the hell am I doing? I ask myself, not really believing I'm getting seriously involved in a circle I know I'll never get out of. Probably not alive, at least. Anxiety kicks in, making me paranoid about being overheard by the woman's henchmen. I glance around not so subtly, my senses on high alert. Irrationality doesn't stop there as worry pushes me to check my car, looking for any trackers. My heart pounds in my ears. The urgency increases, further and *further* just as War's voice comes through the phone.

"Already?" he asks, surprised to hear from me so soon.

A chill runs through me when I finally decide the Nissan is safe and climb inside. I have to take a second to answer, still panting for air because of the adrenaline rush. The chemicals feel *good,* but exhausting. "I don't understand," I declare, confused. "The wedding you sent me to, it was Maddox Ryder's, right? I thought he was the boss around here."

"One of them," War responds monotonously. With him, it's always been challenging to know whether he's vague on purpose to keep people away from what he knows or if he genuinely doesn't have information. Which again seems unlikely, considering he has eyes and ears through people working for him. "What did you find?" he prompts, steering the conversation back.

I put the phone on speaker to scroll through the picture. The woman's presence is so obvious when I look at her image. She is *radiant, controlled.* My brows furrow on their own as I try to add this new thread to the complicated world I'm shyly stepping into. "There was *someone* at the club. A wom—"

"Hold on," he interrupts sharply. "Come to the garage." His tone is commanding, and the order catches me off guard because it's so unusual. For obvious reasons, he tends to keep our interactions to a minimum. When it comes to reporting on a mission, we always have to do it in person. If he's worried about someone eavesdropping, it could mean drawing the attention of his enemies and finding myself in a crossfire. Which is definitely not what I imagined when I started working for him. The supposedly *safe* tasks suddenly feel risky. Despite my confusion, there's no arguing as he hangs up on me.

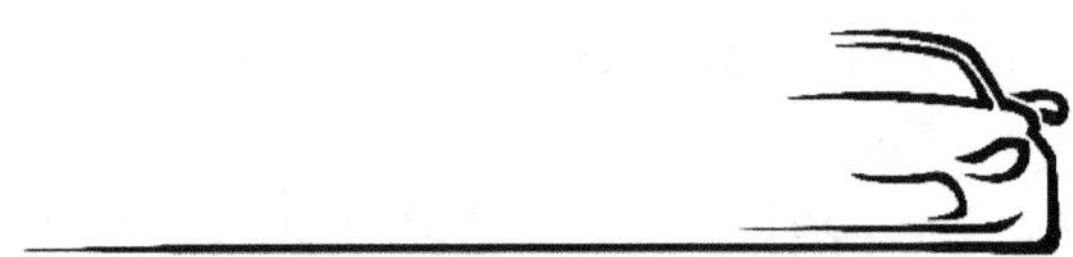

It's mid-afternoon when I eventually arrive in Ursley. The traffic between cities was way worse than I expected. The light of the sun cast a soft yellow glow, slightly blinding me as I drive on the familiar highway leading to the campus. After a stressful morning, I finally relax and bob my head to the rhythm of my music. I hum, trying to forget about what's coming next, but abruptly the car loses power.

"*Wha—*" I glance around, puzzled. Panicked drivers honk at me. The mess in my head is getting worse until I slump in my seat, trying to make myself as small as possible, realizing what's behind this sudden failure. Then it hits me: *I* made a mistake.

The mods I installed on my own just three days ago were supposed to *improve* my car, not make it worse. I'm only three miles away from the garage, and the turbocharger chooses this moment to quit? Naively, I hoped to avoid paying too much for the 240SX by buying from the aftermarket and doing the upgrades myself, thinking that learning from a few videos might have been enough, but I guess that's not the case.

I pull over to the side. As soon as I open my door, a rich oil scent stings my nose. The sweet purr of the engine is now replaced by a deathly silence. Six hundred and seventy-five dollars go up in smoke. I probably could have noticed the issue sooner if only I'd pushed the car a little harder. Driving below the limit must have masked the problem and the long, uninterrupted drive from Greensburg to Ursley exposed it.

"No, no, plea— Shit!" I complain, then curse under my breath, realizing how badly I've screwed up and how the repairs will probably cost me more than the money I'd wanted to save. Fumbling for my phone safely behind the security barrier, I bite my nails. War will think I'm stupid, maybe even start to look for my replacement when I *thought* I was being smart with my choices. *Damn it.* I'm bitter. Angry, I can't even look at my reflection in the passenger window.

When he picks up the call, I don't give him time to say a word, choosing to apologize—once again. "Sorry, you must be waiting for me. My—uh—" I stutter, embarrassed and wishing I would simply disappear.

"What?" my boss utters. Maybe it's my nerves speaking, but I understand this single word as a way to tell me he's had enough and is looking for a reason why this job should be my last.

I sigh, my shoulders slump as my self-confidence evaporates. "My car broke down near the exit to the science buildings. I need a lift."

He grunts in acknowledgement. "Riley!" he yells at someone in the background. "Get me Riley," War orders to one of his mechanics, probably. "I'll get one of my guys to get you with a tow truck."

"Thanks—" Unsurprisingly, the end of the call cuts me off.

Back in my car, waiting patiently, I spot the tow truck in my rear-view mirror. They got here quicker than I thought, but then again, the garage isn't that far. For safety's sake, I step over the console to get out through the passenger side, just in time for War's man to pull up right in front of my pride and joy.

As the man finds me at the back of his vehicle, I instantly recognize the heavily tattooed guy I met several months ago. His features are as dreamy as they were under the moon. "You must be Riley," I greet, smiling kindly.

"The driver," he exclaims charmingly, looking at me then my 240SX. "Nice car." He grins, extending his wrist for a handshake, his hands still coated in grease he evidently hasn't had time to clean off. "I'm Aidan, by the way. Riley had something urgent to take care of."

I nod in understanding—having to drop off everything for *me* is not something I'd force on anyone. "Jade. Thank you—for rescuing me. I guess."

"No problem, Jade. You got me an extended break, so it's a win for me, too." He winks, and I have to lower my head to hide from his attention. The embarrassment still crippling my senses.

I get out of his way and watch as he works on attaching my car to the metal wire. Then, Aidan walks to the side of the truck to activate the mechanism using the commend buttons. He watches absentmindedly, the movements and tasks familiar enough that it doesn't need his full attention. Looking at him is truly a show on itself.

"Here for another job?" he asks over his shoulder as he secures my Nissan in place.

I purse my lips and fidget with my hands nervously. The contrast between his confidence and my restlessness intensifies as I think about all the drivers passing by, watching me, observing what's happening. I *know* they make assumptions, ask questions—what did *I* do wrong? And the self-awareness that's always been a concern for me weighs on my mind. It's something I'm actively working on. The little voice in my head is not my enemy, but it's a little annoying, I have to admit.

"Yes. A report, actually," I answer. Despite the inconvenience of my car breaking down, I can't help but enjoy the sight of Aidan at work, turning a frustrating moment into an entertaining twist. I may not have romantic relationships in mind, but that doesn't stop me from recognizing attraction when I feel it. The dark, mid-length hair, the playful demeanor, the small frame, and clothes full of grease. I never asked myself if I had a type, and yet, apparently, it's *this* kind of guy.

"It never stops, right?"

Shaking my head, I focus on his hypnotizing eyes, caught off guard by my shameless staring. "Sorry?"

But Aidan doesn't mention my rudeness. He turns his head back around attempting, maybe, to give me time to memorize his frame. "Working for War. It never stops. He always has something. You might be a lost little pup, but the second you run to him, he'll find something to keep you busy. A bone to gnaw." He chuckles to himself. The reaction giving me enough to guess he was once this *lost little pup.*

Shrugging, I make my way to the passenger door of his truck, ready to go. My hand rests on the handle, and I take a moment to study his profile. His strong jaw clenches slightly as he focuses on putting everything back in order. "Yes, I know that feeling," I reply, injecting a hint of double-meaning. Without my boss, I don't know what kinds of jobs I might have taken on to cover the expenses. I hop in before he has time to answer.

The interior screams '*garage vehicle*'—oil stains, empty cans, and dirty rags scattered around. Not to mention the tools lying under my feet. Still, I'm grateful they didn't leave me on the side of the road to fend for myself.

Aidan slams the driver's door shut when he finally gets in. The purr of the powerful engine mixed with the heaviness of the truck makes my ears ring as he turns on the ignition. The noise of busy roads is mostly masked by gear shifts, the rumble when he accelerates, and the static sound of the radio playing in the background. Smelling the gasoline fumes calms my mind. It's strange, but that's always been the case.

"So, what happened with the lady in the back?" Aidan inquires simultaneously as he takes the exit that's supposed to bypass the campus, instead of the usual route I take.

I snort at the nickname. My Nissan isn't a *lady*, it's a spoiled princess. "She's not the problem, I am." Facing his frown, I know it'll be hard to escape the interrogation. "I thought I could handle some mods on my own. I bought a kit and *tried* to install it, but..." I shake my head instead of telling him the sentence in full.

"It's the first time?" The absence of judgment in his tone is reassuring. He doesn't treat me like I've done something terribly wrong, and I really appreciate that. Or, he's just being friendly.

I nod. "Everyone starts somewhere, right? Besides, it's my first—well, my second car—but the first I'm building from scratch."

He whistles to show he's genuinely impressed. "A project car without experience? Damn, that's cool," he praises which makes a warm feeling bloom in my stomach.

As he opens his window, I'm hypnotized, watching his charcoal-colored hair dance all over his face.

He tries to tame his unruly strands while steering, amusingly failing and earning a chuckle from me. "I grew up around cars, it's always been on my mind. I knew as soon as I had a bit of money, I'd start something like that," I reveal.

"She's a driver, she builds her own car, she works for War... What else are you hiding, Jade?" He peers at me out of the corner of his eye, a teasing yet cheeky expression on his face. He reaches out to turn off the radio, the volume of which is already low.

I don't answer with words, but a smile that's enough to calm the tension in my body. "What about you? You can't be *only* working at a garage," I joke, watching the road ahead as we make the last turn to reach War's property.

"You're right. I run an illegal fighting ring in Ursley," he states seriously. Despite my frowning, I don't show any reaction which pushes him to turn his head to me when he finally parks the truck in front of a Subaru missing its doors for some reason. For the next seconds, we stay still, staring into each other's eyes. He rests his wrist at the top of the steering wheel and relaxes into the seat. Crossing my arms, I raise a brow, playing along this meaningless eye-contact game we've apparently decided to stretch.

Noticing the bedroom look he's giving me, I burst out laughing. "Sure, give me a heads up for the next match. I'd like to see that," I retort and look away, losing the game.

He answers with a seductive chuckle before he unbuckles his seatbelt and jumps out of the truck. "I'll put you on the VIP list."

Entering the garage, I'm right behind him when the eyes of the other mechanics quickly find mine, studying me as if I were an intruder. Some even stop working to watch my every move. Customers rarely cross the workshop threshold, preferring the office lounge. As for people doing all sorts of missions for War, we usually show up at night. In the short time I've been here, I've noticed that a different team works the evening shift. Maybe both crews are chosen to bridge the gap between the illegal and the legitimate.

Staying close to Aidan as he grabs a water bottle, I manage to avoid the attention that triggers my defensive instincts. "Thank you," I say as he hands one to me.

A guy approaches, a welcoming expression on his face. He nods in greeting and ignores Aidan leaning against the table. "I'm Bradley," he introduces himself, extending his wrist the same way my savior did earlier.

I can't help but wince subtly at the man's attempt to strike up a conversation. One that I hope will be cut short as his flirty gaze makes me uncomfortable. "Jade, nice to meet you."

Beside us, Aidan clears his throat. "Brad, if War finds you talking instead of working, he'll fire you. Like the last time, remember?" he remarks, his tone almost patronizing, which is not what I expect as Bradley seems to be a decade older than him.

Brad gives him a mocking grin, then his face morphs into defiance. Instead of replying with animosity, he redirects his focus back to me. "*Managers...*" He sighs, shaking his head, smiling too, as if inviting me to join in the joke at Aidan's expense.

Caught in the middle, I giggle nervously, unsure of how to react. The tense atmosphere is thankfully interrupted as the boss finally appears at the end of the room. His booming voice, charged with masculine energy, cuts through the heaviness of the air. "Jade, come here," he commands. The sudden call startles me, while Aidan leaps to his feet and Bradley lowers his head in submission. Part of me finds it amusing because when the boss snarls, the sheep scatter. War isn't *just* in charge, he's the whole system, and if one day he wants to tear it down, no one can stand in his way.

I flash a brief, tight-lipped smile at Aidan and hurry toward War, who clearly lacks patience.

trust me

CHAPTER 3
War's Garage in Ursley.

Night has finally settled in, and it's getting pretty cold. The locals have all retreated for the night, and things are quieting down. But because the garage is in a calmer area than the student buildings, the distant sounds of parties blend into the background. It's easy to forget they're even there.

War left soon after our meeting. Obviously, the photos I showed him from the club got him interested. Even through the usual wary look, I saw that spark of curiosity—a new secret about Maddox Ryder he hasn't cracked yet. Something that fuels his need for more info.

My boss is convinced this woman has no ties to the people he's targeting with his spies. How he figured it out is a mystery, but he probably keeps a file on every person within a thousand-mile radius. Each with their designated folder locked away in his office—records similar to what he must keep of me. Apparently, this woman is a new addition to the web of loyalties and strained relationships. That's all he told me when I pushed for more details out of sheer nosiness.

But the most important part isn't just knowing—it's understanding what happens around me and which side I'm on. The one that'll help me become someone I'm proud of. Learning to be loyal, to keep going, and to accept my past to move on has always been a struggle I knew I couldn't solve alone. Even though I still try my hardest to be an exception.

War must know what happened to me. He has to. Teaching me the value of loyalty and making me want to prove myself is his chosen method. He ignites my competitiveness all the while showing me how being reliable can pay off.

It's more than just a lesson, it's his way of molding me into a stronger asset. After all, living with secrets, War has skillfully turned them into his weapon of choice. And us—his drivers—into dogs ready to run for him. It's not so bad when the outcome is more fulfilling than anything else. But now that I realize it, I'll have to work twice as hard not to lose myself and become his brainless puppet.

Even more so today when the simple '*Good job, Jade,*' when I gave him what he wanted made my day. The points I scored brought a smile to my face and a sense of pride. This mission was a success. Beyond the much-needed cash, I saw in War's gaze my profile has been moved a little further above the other drivers. But now, there's no room for mistakes. With the car out for the rest of the night, it means saying goodbye to my app. Though, even if I'm trying to avoid it, War's jobs are undoubtedly my only chance to cover the repair costs.

Most of the mechanics have left, leaving me almost alone in the neon-lit garage. The boss offered a car as long as I chose his guys to fix my Nissan, but this place, being one of the most popular, charges way more than the regular one I usually visit for my oil change. It's not my place to ask for a discount, he's made it clear his managers handle the operations.

Between the car lifts, tire-fitting station, and welding equipment, Aidan's deep into his to-do list, a pencil clenched between his teeth.

"Do you even sleep at night?" I interrupt him.

He straightens up at the sound of my voice and immediately greets me with a smile. "Do you?" he counters.

I pretend to think about it, looking off into the distance. "It happens." Walking closer, I scan the car currently on the hydraulic machine. Since I'm trying my hardest to learn about mechanical issues on my own, I test my knowledge by spotting the signs that suggest the need to look under the chassis. "It's missing an exhaust system," I conclude, checking over my shoulder for his confirmation. Feeling somewhat concerned about being wrong.

Aidan, who hasn't looked away from my back, approaches slowly. His eyes, two onyx gems, hold me like a prisoner as the empty space between us disappears progressively. My heart's pounding, I read it as excitement, but the shivers that run through me, which usually start just before a race, tell me it's anxiety. The last time I had this much focus on me it was under terrible circumstances. My body, remembering the horrible emotion, forces me to take a step back.

"It is. The owner loves to go off-road with a car clearly not meant for that. He crossed a river, and was surprised some parts rotted or got damaged afterward." Aidan snorts, rolling his eyes at the level of stupidity. "Vince is in charge of that one." He nods at the car overhead. "He had to replace almost all of it. A rock pierced the exhaust."

"Vince is taking care of it alone?" It'd be very unusual since this type of work needs many hands. One mechanic handling it alone would take *weeks.*

"No. The others come to help him when he needs it. But when we can, only one of us takes care of a customer. That way, we can handle more work." Moving around me, he casually drops the to-do list and crosses his arms over his chest. Leaning on the table nearby, his gaze focus on me with an unmistakable glimmer in his eyes. There's a slight tilt to his head and a sultry curl to his mouth. Maybe it's the late hour or the fact that we're alone, but I find myself enjoying this moment with him. It reminds me of how it was like to be with a friend.

I mirror his behavior, moistening my lips with intentional slowness. I steal a glance at the curious shapes of his tattoos, tracing the contours of his body. Embracing the movements of his limbs. The ink is so dark it's visible through his white shirt.

"Which car is yours? If managers also have clients." I glance around, briefly giving him my back as I decide to explore elsewhere. The soft tapping of his shoes replaces the faint sounds of the city. I stop in front of a sleek European convertible, which brand I don't recognize.

His steps become louder, hinting at his closeness. My body tenses, determined not to show any attraction. Anticipation builds in my core as I wonder what he'll do next. My senses heighten, and I feel him halt right behind me. My breath quickens, making me open my mouth to let in more air, the eagerness building with every second.

With feather-like touches, he gently guides my chin to the left with his warm fingers. His hand lingers, offering a comfort I had forgotten. "Civic Type R," he murmurs in my right ear, his lips leaving a soft caress.

"JDM," I whisper back, afraid that if I speak louder it would break the tension between us.

His thumb strokes my cheek for a second before he breaks contact. A puff of hot air from his mouth makes my hair dance over my shoulder. "These are the best. Don't you think, Jade?" The smile in his voice is unmistakable. I turn on myself, hoping to catch the expression before it fades.

Aidan's body is pressed against mine, the mischievous grin I've been expecting still on his face. "What do *you* drive?" I ask, trying to sound flirty. The awkward rasp makes me cringe, but he doesn't seem to have noticed.

"RX-7," he announces proudly.

My mouth drops open, eyes widening with interest. "No way," I exclaim, unable to contain my enthusiasm. "Did you know it was my favorite car when I was little?" Memories flood back of my father and I watching a documentary on a rally driver who owned a Mazda. I fell in love with the style of this car back then—the soft lines, the iconic retractable headlights.

The mechanic glances around us, leaning slightly to peer past the vehicles. "Let's go for a ride," he offers. The temptation is too great, but reason urges me to question if he should be working instead. Yet, the allure is too strong, and I can't resist accepting.

"You'll be okay?" I'm still hesitant because I don't want to cause him trouble.

He winks playfully, takes my hand, and drags me toward one of the five garage doors. On the wall, a control panel catches my attention. "I'll close everything. The guys working at night should be there any minute now, but they have the codes." He flips some switches, and instantly, the doors roll down. Metallic scraping echoes through the room, making my teeth clench to prevent shivering. The sound is like a fork screeching on a chalkboard.

Aidan scribbles a note and leaves it by the entrance. As his eyes lock onto mine again, I feel the intensity and giddiness in them, reaching out and touching me, making me pliant. "Ready?" He's giving me the opportunity to change my mind, yet could I? His gaze only makes me greedy for his attention, stirring a desire catching me off guard—too sudden, too fast.

I nod shyly as his hand rests on the small of my back, guiding me out of the garage. We walk around the parking lot, finally reaching the RX-7 whose color is hard to distinguish under the dim lighting. My expression brightens at finally being able to see a car that's been in my dreams for years. I crouch in front of it, extending my hand to touch the body. Aidan is patient—snorting at my antics, but patient.

"I've never seen one in real life," I confess, breathless, finally standing up to walk around it. Taking out my phone to turn on the light, I see the Mazda in detail. The paint is as black as the night sky, shimmering in the light. He has custom copper rims and did a neat job with the fenders to accommodate the size of his *massive* tires.

"It's—" I shake my head at a loss for words, looking at him. "It's perfect."

Aidan stands tall, pleased, hands in his jeans, and an attractive smirk on his lips, clearly enjoying the compliments. I know the feeling well—the satisfaction when my work is praised. "I've been working on it for over five years now. It's worth *every* dollar."

"You did it *yourself?*" I ask, stunned—not because it's strange that a mechanic can do it, but because I know for sure what's under the hood isn't entirely *legal.* When you have the knowledge and skills, nothing is impossible. I can already imagine the g-force pressing me into the seat as he speeds on the highway.

He nods. "Except for the paint job."

Leaving him on the side, I resume my inspection. The exhaust is close enough to touch the ground, and the rear wing further emphasizes its beast-like appearance. He even installed a twin-turbo setup which adds to my shock. "It's insane. It looks like one of those Japanese kits," I point out, noting the similarities with the wide body kit style people often go for—*myself included.*

Aidan joins me back at the front. Both of us facing the car. "I got inspired by it. But no, I didn't buy one. I have everything customized exactly how I want it." He exhales audibly before circling around me, his right arm draping over my shoulders as he takes me to the passenger door. He opens it swiftly, flashing a dazzling grin, then trots to the driver's seat on the right side of the car. A giggle escapes me, though I mask the expression and hide my hands under my legs.

When he starts the engine and revs it, making it roar, my grin spreads. I find it amusing he clearly wants to show off.

"Ready, little driver?" he teases, his voice low.

I jerk my head to him, revealing two straight rows of teeth. "Ready."

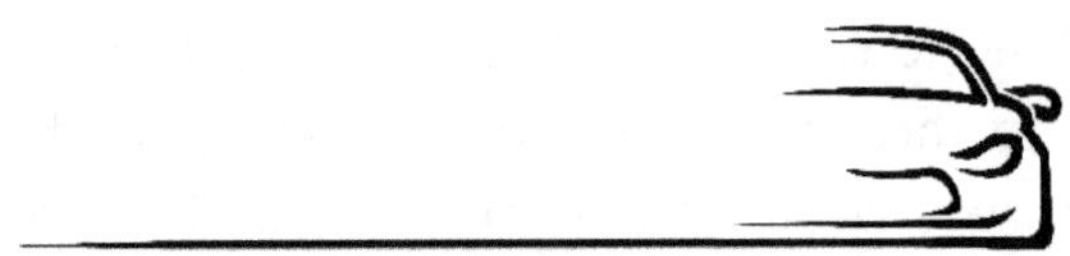

My hands grip the seatbelt tightly, my breathing is fast and uneven. The RX-7 is unleashed on the Ursley campus. Aidan takes us to the outskirts of the city, testing the limits of how much freedom the authorities would allow in the dead of night.

Trusting him with my life may be the stupidest decision I've ever made, but the speed, the adrenaline rush—emotions I never thought I could experience from the passenger side—make me realize that in *this* moment, I'm grateful for the faith I've placed in *him*. He skillfully controls the car, assuming the driver's role while I become the customer for once.

He steers the wheel, and the Mazda responds instantly. The rear locks briefly, making the tires scraping the asphalt before releasing, allowing the car to drift effortlessly through the turn. I'm jealous of his ease, he has done a better job than I ever did in my street racing career. Seeing him controlling the car as if they were one is also pretty attractive. Someone never looked this *good* doing it.

"Aidan!" I yell, a mix of half-complaint, half-terror. My body tenses and relaxes with each calculated move. The outside world turns into streaks of light as the speed increases. Yet under the layer of fear, there's this genuine excitement. His carefree personality makes this the best night of my life.

"You okay, little driver?" he asks, amused by my alarmed look.

"Ye—" I yelp when he avoids the only other car on the road. "You're going to get us ki—"

"Nuh-uh," he interrupts before the word gets out. "*Feel,*" he instructs. And I'm suddenly awestruck by the colors blending together. The outside becomes an abstract painting of only straight lines. The vibrations remind me of the power under the hood. *How much power that may be? Six-hundred? Seven? What about the torque?*

My heart skips a beat at the feel of his palm on my thigh. Only there to grab the flesh, to get my attention back on him.

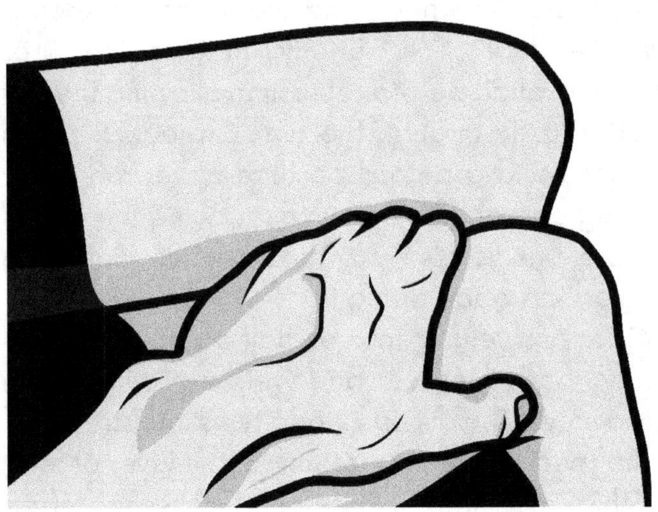

I examine his tattooed fingers, each bearing a letter. When combined, they don't spell out any words. On the back of his hand, a caged bird with snapped wings is surrounded by barbed wires. A strange art, yet fitting for his character.

"Do you feel that?" Eyes on the road ahead, he seems to have forgotten about the brake pedal altogether.

The attraction? The need inside of me? "What?" I ask.

"The pounding of your heart telling you you're about to die?"

In the night, everything is allowed, it's a rule that only the most reckless drivers follow. The endless possibilities make my blood boil with passion, *desire*. The pressure to take without limit is addictive for us. It *does* feel like dying.

My gaze locks with Aidan's, and in this silent dialogue, there's an unspoken understanding—he feels the same. "What else?" I breathe out, almost too softly. In answer, his grip tightens on my thigh, enough to leave bruises. Every emotion comes at me, all at once. The tip of his fingers on my inner thigh guides me further in this euphoric state.

"Close your eyes. Trust me." His voice is gentle, coaxing, so I do. I close them and press my palms over their sockets. "Tell me how it feels."

I smile to myself, but focus on his commands. As I open my mouth to tell him about my near cardiac arrest, he opens the windows, letting the freezing air in. The next instant, he stomps on the throttle. The powerful engine roars, mixing with the howling wind. Rapid rush of air with its high-pitched whistles tears a scream out of my throat. There are no limits. "It doesn't feel real. It's like, I'm not inside my body anymore," I scream for my voice to carry over the whoosh.

Aidan handles the twists and turns like a pro. His hand never leaves my thigh, reassuring me that he knows what he's doing.

"What about now, Jade?" His tone matches mine, dancing with the wind to reach my ears. His lighthearted tone brings a bigger grin on my face. Leaning back against the headrest, I keep my hands shielding my eyes while he continues to play with the car, smoothly rocking it from side to side. My body shakes with the movements and churns my stomach. On instinct, I reach out to him for comfort. As his fingers entwine with mine and grip tightly, a wild laugh erupts from me. The sound is genuine and carefree, washing away the nervousness from earlier.

"It's like I'm on a roller coaster," I reply finally.

Gradually, the car comes to a stop which tightens my seatbelt against my body. "Where are we?" I ask, my senses deprived of his touch, leave me in the dark.

He sighs, as if he has just finished a good workout, satisfied with his efforts. On my cheek, I feel the warmth of his knuckles brushing against my face. I hold my breath in anticipation. Parting my lips subtly, I extend my tongue to moisten them, but—

"You can open your eyes now," he murmurs into my ear. I comply, my gaze automatically looking for his. What I see is the aftermath of the excitement, leaving only the passion and the need to get closer. In the blink of an eye, Aidan seizes my face, squeezes my cheeks, and his lips crash into mine.

He kisses me eagerly and I match his enthusiasm. Aidan's mouth moves confidently. It's sweet and hot, while his touch is intense and devouring. My hands cling to his wrist while his thumb draws circles on my ears. I love the sounds we make. My tongue dances with his, mirroring his own strokes. I chase after him, stretching my legs and pushing myself up to be closer. He inhales sharply, and I take the opportunity to catch his lower lip between mine. I nibble and suck without a care, not stopping when he smiles. His hands, first on my face, move possessively to the nape of my neck to keep me firmly attached to him. Following his lead, I fold my legs over the seat, straightening on my knees, and hover over him, nearly falling into his lap because of my arousal.

"Ja—" He tries to speak, but his words are drowned out, leaving only the sounds of pleasure fill the air.

In one swift move, he grabs my waist and easily lifts me onto his lap. Straddling him on the driver's side, I put distance between our faces to show him the smile stretching my muscles. Not having had enough, I try to taste him again, but his fist on my hair stops me.

"Have you looked around us, little driver?" he remarks, fully aware I've been distracted, my focus consumed by his heart-eyes and those plump lips calling out for me.

I pinch mine together, trying to hide my amusement. I should be embarrassed at my lack of control, but it doesn't really matter. "Why should I?" I retort, placing a kiss on the tip of his straight nose.

He makes a non-committal sound, acknowledging my point. "True, though—" He cuts his sentence short, his gaze shifting between my lips, eyes, and nose. As if, like me, nothing else matters when the fog clouds our brains. A colorful stream of curse words spills from him as he grabs my hair and pulls my head back, crashing our lips together again. The taste—a mix of him and a hint of nicotine—is unexpectedly addictive. How could I enjoy the taste of alcohol when this guy makes me just as drunk?

"Please, get out of the car before I lock us inside," Aidan urges.

For a brief moment, neither of us moves, just drowning in each other's presence. "Maybe, you should release me?" I tease him, bringing his attention to the arm holding my body firmly against his torso and the fist still tangled in my hair.

He playfully rolls his eyes at being caught, then tightens his grip instead of letting go. Without breaking eye contact, he opens the door and gently leans my face against his shoulder to protect me from the low roof. I wrap my arms and legs around him and breathe in his scent at the same time, a mixture of motor oil and fuel that my brain now associates with the mechanic.

Slowly, he sets me down. Only then do I notice our surroundings and I can't help but gasp.

CHAPTER 4

Near Ursley.

The fog hangs in the air, and the dim yellow street lights give the empty road a weird mood. I glance at him but quickly turn around to look behind me—the Mazda is parked in the middle of a bridge. Darkness and complete silence surround us. His lips are so captivating that I didn't even notice the lack of sound.

The scene feels surreal, like the emotions I get listening to a certain type of music at three in the morning. Aidan walks past me, smirking over his shoulder as I stand there, stunned. "Come on, let me show you something," he says, holding out his arm.

Hesitant, I grasp his pinky and ring finger in a fist, making sure he can't leave me alone in the middle of nowhere. "Aidan, where are we?" I ask, my voice low but clear in the still night.

"Before the main roads were built to connect the cities, this used to be the only way in Ursley. There's barely any traffic anymore. People have forgotten about this place," he reveals, staring into the distance. He leads me to the edge of the bridge, in front of the protective barrier and moves my chin to the scene below—a calm river with a forest on each side. Normally, the height would give me vertigo, but with Aidan here my thoughts quiet.

"It's beautiful," I whisper, the words aren't enough to describe the landscape. "Thank you for bringing me here." Glancing at him, I try to memorize his expression, his eyes.

"You're welcome." Turning on his feet, he gently raises our hands to kiss my knuckles and sends a wink my way.

I feel a slight shiver as I watch him, as I examine his arms, the hair swaying across his face, the charming freckles beneath the ink of his cheeks, the mole above the one on his forehead. Aidan is both handsome and charming.

When the sun sets and the moon rises, when the wind picks up and the fog settles, when darkness surrounds us and stars appear, it's a moment I hold to my heart. I often take time for granted, whether I'm driving around or working. *There is still tomorrow,* I always tell myself. A new day to turn my life around. But, when those hours come and I'm lost in thoughts, I *wish* the past hadn't happened. It's the what-ifs that always come and I can't control. What if the accident never happened? What if I had friends?

The space between Aidan and me feels too big, so I rise on my tiptoes and cup his face in my hands, showing him this *what-if* will never be. Because in the night nothing is real, everything is possible, and I can be whoever I want.

I silently ask for permission with my eyes, and when I catch the glimmer of light in his, I brush my lips over his. His hands find my waist, pulling me closer, then he lifts me for a more intense kiss. Gently, he runs his fingers through my hair with a grin as a surprised sound escapes me. "So fucking cute," he murmurs against my skin, his hands gripping my bottom.

My arms, which were around his neck, drop to grab his elbows. The next second, my legs wrap around his waist, and my worry spikes. My breath quickens as he turns around to guide my back against the bridge barrier.

"Aidan—" I breathe out, uncertainty and fear tainting my voice.

He silences me with a hush, pressing his pelvis against mine to hold our position. "You're fine, don't worry" he whispers, reassuring while his palms glide up and down my thighs. The edge presses against my shoulder blades. "You're fine," he repeats, kissing each of my cheeks between words. I nod, trusting him. Eager to continue, I lean in and moisten my lips, hooding my eyes with lust.

"I like when you do that."

"Wha—"

Aidan, supporting my body, presses against me more strongly. Mirroring what I did, he runs his tongue over my mouth. *"This."* I feel a blush spreading across my face and I'm sure he would've noticed it if the light had been brighter.

The pulse in my veins intensifies and a hunger sweeps through me as his hands explore beneath my dress, sliding over my stockings to feel my bottom. My lips part, releasing a breathy plea. He lowers his head to the crook of my neck. "Your skin is so soft. I can feel your pulse on my lips."

"Please." My skin tingles under his touch. On instinct, I push of my chest forward. The warm breath, mixed with the movement of his hips against mine, overwhelms me in a way that has me thinking I'm somebody else.

I'm not Jade anymore, I think to myself. *I can be whoever I want in my dreams.* This moment is too magical to be real.

My shins press against Aidan's thighs, silently encouraging him to deepen his thrusts. Understanding my silent need, he stops the friction and lowers me to the ground. My dress rides up my waist to reveal my thong. I expect him to undress me, but he surprises me by pinching the hem and smoothly drags it down.

Taking a step back, he breaks all contact between our bodies. "You might get cold," he states, his jaw clenched, barely meeting my gaze. At first, I think he's changed his mind. We may be alone, lost in a fantasy, but maybe I'm not the one he wants. Then, my eyes catch the obvious arousal in his pants. Though quickly, I remember that men can show attraction without desire. Yet, Aidan brought me here, started all this. If he didn't want me, he wouldn't have done it.

But after all, it's all about communication. Words hold every power. "I'm not," I say with a slight frown, trying to tell him I'm good without being awkward. "I like it. If that's what you want. Then, me too." We're adults, and wanting a physical relationship isn't inherently wrong—it never was, especially when both parties consent.

"Are you sure?" Aidan respects my boundaries and refrains from swaying me with his touch.

Grinning, I adopt a seductive look. "I am."

"You'll tell me if you change your mind, right?" He gets closer once again, hesitantly raising his hands. He bites his lip to contain the enjoyment, but fails when I grab his shirt to pull him toward me.

"I will," I promise before crashing my lips onto his. As I had hoped, Aidan reciprocates the kiss, holding my face in place as his tongue moves in a circular motion. The tension builds once again, and I'm determined to never let him go. Lifting one of my legs to bring our pelvises closer, he caves and holds onto my knee.

Gone is the restraint from before, *this* is the man losing control. The electricity that hits our skin when we touch gives me goosebumps, adding to the sensations as I rub against his erection with more insistence. I can feel the wetness building up in my underwear. Moans escape our lips and we work in unison for our mutual pleasure. Panting and moaning, we stare into each other's eyes, lost in passion.

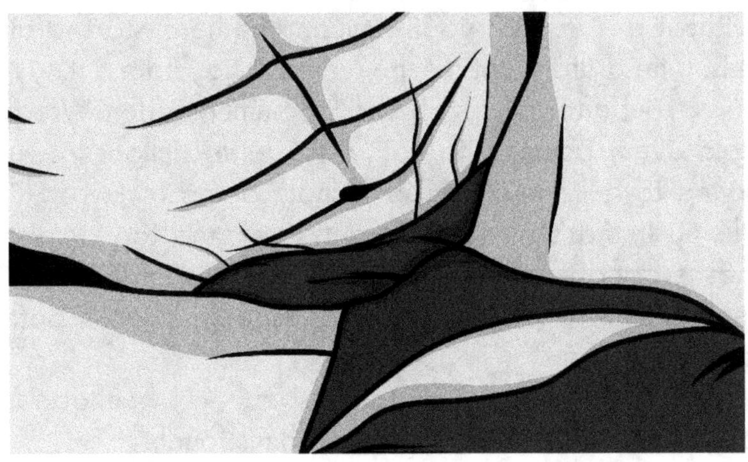

His hand, the one that holds my jaw in place, travels down my throat to my breasts. He caresses their roundness, loves their softness. In a rush, I open my dress from the back and lower the piece of clothing to my waist, allowing my skin to come into contact with the fresh air. It's not uncomfortable. If anything, it slows my pace and reminds me that, even if it looks surreal, this dream is reality.

My bra does a poor job of concealing my erect nipples. "Take it off," I urge him, losing my mind over the sensitivity. A growl rises from his throat, which lets me know he's as desperate as me.

Keeping my leg in his hold, he deftly pinches off the unwanted cover. I take the lingerie from his hand and toss it over the barrier into the water.

"Why did you do that?" He snorts at my impulsivity.

Shrugging, I don't really have a reason besides being spontaneous. Trying to distract him, I pull him in again, guiding his lips to mine. His hands skillfully massage my chest before sliding down my stomach to his pants. I feel him increasing the friction between my legs, teasing himself, while his knuckles give my clit the attention it craves.

"Like that, Jade. Like that, *good*," he praises, making me let out a breathy moan. Our foreheads pressed together, his intense gaze locks with mine as he unzips his jeans. Hearing the zipper, I bunch up my dress at my back, keeping it on in case someone might finally appear on that bridge and we'll have to run. "I need you inside of me, Aidan."

"I know. I *know*, sweetheart." He lowers his pants just below his hips, like me, leaves his underwear on for now. Lifting my knee up to his waist, he clings on to my thigh, preventing any escape, while his other hand grips my soft flesh, controlling our movements more effectively. The position presses every inch of me against him, and I reach back, gripping the chain-link fence.

"God, how does it feel so damn good," he rasps. "Do you see how your pussy calls me. *Fuck.*"

My mouth opens in a gasp as he eagerly rubs against me, stimulating my needy sex. My muscles clench with every wave of passion. I throw my head back, trying to inhale as much air as I can.

"Do you have protection?" I ask breathlessly. My desires are soaring, and at this moment, I know not even a passerby could make me let go of him.

Aidan slows down, both of us cursing under our breaths as we feel his cock effortlessly tease my slit through my panties. The air makes the wet patch on my crotch turn impossibly freezing which intensifies the already overwhelming sensations. *"Fuck,"* he mutters. "It's in the car."

I need to concentrate so I don't scream in frustration. Knowing he'll have to leave my arms to get what we need is absolutely annoying. Unconsciously, my leg tightens around him and a loud moan escapes me. "Aidan. Aidan, *oh*—" I call his name like a prayer as his thrusts bring me closer to climax.

"I'll get it, Jade," he murmurs in my ear, holding my nape when he kisses my lobe.

In response, without my consent, my hand reaches onto his firm bottom, gripping his muscles to prevent him from going anywhere.

"Let me go," he repeats playfully.

"No, no," I say, helplessly. Realizing what I'm saying, I quickly change my speech. "Yes." I frown and shake my head desperately, trying to let the breeze clear the sex-induced haze clouding my mind.

He frees my leg and leans forward, capturing my pert nipple between his lips. He sucks and rolls the stiff tip with his tongue learning about my reaction at the same time. He flicks them and gently teases with his teeth, sending a delicious throb through me. His eyes meet mine, reading my expression. I'm hooked, and a little scared of how much I crave his attention.

"I'll be right back," he promises against my skin, brushing his nose a last time on my tender buds, making me gasp.

He pulls back completely, raises his pants, and turns around in a swift motion. I observe as he jogs to the car, opens it, and plunges inside.

Nearly naked, in the middle of nowhere, missing his warmth, I finally process what we're doing. I'm not having second thoughts about it. I'm excited and so ready to relieve the tension. If anything, the public place, the risk of getting caught, is even more arousing. I've never done something like that before, something so *wild*.

Once he gets out of the car, Aidan holds up the condom like a trophy.

"Please hurry," I beg, waving my hand at him.

With a teasing smile on his face, he comes back to me, and I don't let him rethink or ask if I'm sure again. Instead, I peck his lips, smirk, and turn around to watch the horizon blend into shades of blues, blacks, and purples. The water below, shining like diamonds, is nearly enough to make me forget I'm not in bed.

Aidan's hand works on himself while I wait, thinking of those rare moments in life where someone finally understands the meaning of being *alive*.

"Like this?" His voice in my ear sends goosebumps on my skin.

Slightly turning my head to the left, I nod. "Like this. I want to watch the sky when I feel you." His hands flatten on my hips, tracing over the diamond pattern of the fishnet stockings, and my panties still in place. Instinctively, I arch my back to feel his touch, wiggling my bottom to fuel his lust. He answers swiftly when he hooks the stockings with his finger at the apex of my legs, ripping them open for better access. I gasp at the bold act but feel the pulse in my vagina double in pace.

"They were in the way," Aidan remarks lightly. He kisses my shoulder, my neck, when I feel the tip of his cock between my legs. They open by themselves as he pulls on my completely wet thong to push it aside. An umpteenth curse escapes him when he realizes my swollen pussy badly needs him—aches for him. He doesn't make me wait any longer, one hand holding my hips in place while the other guides himself to my dripping hole, teasing my cunt a few times. "It's fucking heaven." He runs his shaft along my slit, making sure it's well coated in my slick before he enters my body.

The chill in the air doesn't bother me, not when he dives inside at an agonizing pace. It's driving me mad but brings my mind in sync with his every move. He hums sultrily against my skin, planting kisses on my head and along my neck as he fully thrusts inside of me. Feeling every inch of him is what I love the most. He slides in and out leisurely, letting me adjust to his size before picking up a more primal, intense rhythm.

"Aidan, stop torturing me," I whisper, begging for more. My knuckles turn white from gripping the barrier so hard. My throat is dry because I can't close my mouth, too caught up in my urges to have enough air to fill my lungs.

"But I love torturing you, little driver." Yet Aidan speeds up, his hand on my hip moving around my torso to cup my bare chest. He kneads my flesh possessively, biting my shoulder, and praising me. His hard cock rams into me faster now. The panting growing more urgent. We move in perfect harmony, I meet his thrusts halfway, and together we work as one. Around me, the colors become more vivid, the coldness transforms into warmth, and the sounds of the water is drowned by his heavy breathing in my ear. The insatiable hunger grows, making me drop my head back against his shoulder.

I scream louder.

Aidan loses himself inside of my cunt, and I make sure to savor every stroke of his skin on my sweet spot, teasing my sensitive walls. I become a mess of moans and breathy whimpers. I reach for his hair, grabbing his locks in a fist.

"God, yes, *yes*. Just like that," I sob.

His tongue teases my skin while he plunges into me, deeper, faster. Both of us communicating without words.

Finding a better rhythm, Aidan dives back into me with momentum sending his pelvis crashing into mine, causing my head to bang against the railing. As I inhale and exhale the fresh air, my vision blurs. My body, completely at his mercy, collapses in on itself while he steadies me and takes me without a second thought. Sensing my legs giving out, my knees buckling, I cling to his hands over my chest. Together, we sink on the ground. I'm on all fours while Aidan continues to penetrate me, bending one leg for better support, allowing him to go harder, *fucking me* even more passionately. We create a lewd and dirty, though strangely liberating, moment.

The squelching sounds fill the air, and the slick runs down my legs. The wetness has an ice-cold effect against my burning skin. Our breath turns to vapor, and we moan together.

"You like that, *huh*? Being treated like a slut. Oh, sweetheart you feel so good." Aidan fucks me with greater intensity than before. But in contrast, his arms hold me close. My muscles pulsate around his cock, and the desire to have him inside me forever sounds like the perfect idea.

The asphalt hurts my knees, and I'm sure they'll bleed soon, but nothing matters. In the night, I cry out his name as a sweet, floating sensation takes me by surprise. The moment is a relief. I'm on the brink, but I don't want to stop. I meet his thrusts enthusiastically, taking his length as deep as I can. My legs spread, scraping against the ground, but it *doesn't* matter. Leaning forward, I hook my fingers onto the railing and focus on the moon. My mouth is wide open as I squeal and grunt. This new position finally allows him to go deeper.

Aidan lets go of my sore breast, now holding my waist with one hand and gathering my hair with the other, pulling me onto his cock. He watches closely as I impale myself on him, mesmerized by the way our bodies mold into each other.

Saliva runs down my chin, and my sounds become incoherent as his grow more vulgar, needier, and cruder. I can't process his words, just a nonsensical flow. "Your pussy is heaven, Jade. *My god*, I want to bury my nose in your cunt. I love fucking you under the moon," he grumbles. The arousal reaches a new high, if that's even possible. Aidan explores my body, using me to please himself like his hands would.

I can't breathe anymore. Thoughts mingle, overwhelmed by all the senses. I don't know anything anymore except him inside of me might be the only thing I'll ever need. I grunt, my hands falling to the ground as I wish I could live like this—being fucked with abandon and to not worry about anything else. The magic finally arrives, and my brain floats in a mix of chemicals, similar to a good dose of alcohol. My ears ring as I savor the orgasm coursing through my veins. Blood pounds in my brain, and I gasp for air, letting the trembles pass.

Aidan lets me know he loves how I try to lock him in me, contracting my cunt desperately. Tiredness sets in and desire fades, but Aidan doubles his efforts. His own pleasure pushing him to fuck me until one of us passes out. His movements become wild and, in return, my body submits to his. My neck hurts from the tight angle he holds it at. My hair is in his fist. He thrusts faster, the sounds become more and more lewd. *Clap, clap, clap.* It's ridiculous how much I love this.

One last time he buries himself all the way in, stays there and groans louder. He spills inside the rubber and enjoys, like me, his release.

The fog dissipates fast, leaving only two bodies completely satisfied. I'm breathless, my muscles ache, and the tingling sensation between my legs continues, as well as a slight discomfort. My throat is so dry I can't swallow. I wipe the drool from my chin with the back of my hand. What felt and sounded erotic has now shifted into embarrassment and a hint of disgust.

But I don't regret it. It was perfect.

Aidan slowly pulls out and releases my hair from his grip. He apologizes when he hears the wince I try to hide. "Damn, I'm so sorry. I got carried away—"

"No, it's fine," I reassure him, fully understanding. What I don't want right now is the awkwardness that usually follows. With difficulty, I sit on my haunches and gather my clothes. Aidan fastens his pants, then quickly steps in to help me zip up the back of my dress. "Thank you," I express shyly.

"No problem." He glances around, and I sense the air turning weird. I feel like an idiot, but it doesn't have to be this way. "Here." He takes off his shirt, revealing the intricate work of ink I've been curious about since we met, and hands it to me. "Clean yourself with it until I get you something better," he says, turning away to give me privacy. I rush to clean up and hold his shirt in a ball, unsure what to do with it, so I decide to keep it and clear my throat.

"Are you okay?" he asks, genuine concern on his face.

"Of course," I quickly reply. "Sorry, I didn't want it to be this—"

"Awkward," he completes for me. "Yeah, me either." His expression softens which calms my nerves and with it, the urge to run. "Let me get you inside the car. You must be freezing." Wrapping an arm protectively around my shoulders, he guides me to the passenger side. Taking the shirt from my hands, he gets his jacket from the back of the headrest and lays it across my lap. With a confident slam of the door, I watch in awe as this shirtless man, his skin covered with countless tattoos, hurries around the Mazda to settle into the driver's seat.

A second follows, where we both sit in silence, looking around and lost in thoughts. There's something special about living this with him—the dream I always chase, night after night.

"Jade," he breaks the stillness, capturing my attention. I turn my head toward him and observe as his gaze travels from my eyes to linger on my mouth. The desire to kiss him intensifies but before I can act, he takes the lead and gently cups my cheek. My eyes flutter close as the smoothness of his skin brushes against mine. The blush on my face betrays my emotions, and a shy smile spreads across my lips. His laughter is infectious.

"Would you like to eat something?" he offers, acknowledging we've gone from the garage straight to here. His thumb caresses my jaw, and he can't resist planting another brief kiss on my lips.

"I'm starving, actually," I admit.

"Good. We can go to my place, and I can order something." He fastens his seatbelt and starts the engine, the urge to drive irresistible—I know it well. I agree yet when he glances at me his eyelids narrow as an idea crosses his mind. "How about a deal? You choose whatever you'd like to eat, and you do me a little favor," he states.

"What kind of favor?" I ask hesitantly.

"Do you know how to cut hair?" The question sparks curiosity and can't say I'm not eager to know more.

a little favor

CHAPTER 5

Aidan's Apartment in Ursley.

With confidence in my ability to copy what I saw in the video, I nod and release an anxious breath under Aidan's teasing gaze. He knows I'm more likely to mess up his hair than do a decent job, still, it's what he wants.

"Don't worry, a shave is hardly something complicated to do," he jokes, already prepared for anything. Initially, I suggested we do it in his bathroom where he could guide me through it while I cut, but he needed a cigarette as soon as possible. I realize now that I should have waited to shower until after we entered his flat, as the smell will surely cling to the shirt and boxers he gave me.

I walk up behind him and gently rest my hands on his bare shoulders. He's sitting on a stool by the window, letting the fresh air clear the smell. "Why cutting it? Your hair is gorgeous…" I run my fingers through the dark charcoal strands, feeling a bit sad at the thought of having to cut all of it. It suits him perfectly and the length really adds to his charm. "I think you should *really* give this some thought."

As I brush my fingers through it, massaging his scalp, he drops his head back to rest it on my stomach. I observe his closed eyes, the ink over them. What I initially thought was gibberish actually makes perfect sense. The words '*dead*' and '*end*' are meant to be read upside down. It's a strange choice, but one that fits his character.

He opens his eyes, an unfamiliar emotion visible in his irises. "It's like a tradition. I made a promise," he reveals. He hesitates, wondering if he should say more. After a deep breath, he straightens up. "It's a stupid rule we invented with my friends when we were kids. Where I come from, there's not much of a future. It's always drugs or prison. Most of the time, it's both. So, when one of us got caught in either, we all had to shave or get a tattoo that reminded us of them." He takes a drag of his cigarette, looking outside the window. He snorts when he realizes how it sounds now that he's an adult. "It's stupid."

I eye his tattoos, noting their number. Are they all reminders? Proof of the promise? If so, I can't imagine how difficult it must be to stay strong when most of the people you grew up with are *gone*. It's tragic but it's *his* story. We're strangers, but I appreciate him telling me this. "I don't think it is. It's good you've kept this promise all this time." We're not so different when it comes to vows. It's a little like me and how I gave up alcohol.

Shifting closer to his body, I press my front against his back, raising my hands to his scalp to resume the massage. "Did you grow up in Ursley?" I ask softly.

"Yes. I've been here all my life, but I like this city. Even though it's starting to be invaded by mafia problems." Remembering his host duties, Aidan jerks his head back and offers his cigarette to me, which I refuse with the back of my hand. "Right, I remember. You don't smoke."

"I tried in the past, but the taste is horrible," I state, a grimace contorting my features.

Puffing the last of his white cloud out of his mouth, he crushes the butt on the frame. A gentle expression on his face, he pivots on the stool to face me and takes my legs between his thighs. His hands naturally find their place on my hips as he raises his chin to look at me. I try to read the words written on his cheek, but the street-graffiti-like art style makes the letters unrecognizable.

"So, if I want to kiss you right now, will you refuse?" he teases, knowing my body has already started to melt from his attention alone.

I shake my head and part my lips slightly. His hands become bold, kneading the flesh of my bottom under the men's shorts. He quickly moves his palms under the shirt, lifting the polyester material and smiling innocently, teasing me when there's only an inch left before the under of my breasts are exposed.

My hands rest on his shoulders, lightly tracing the drawings on his skin with my fingers. "I just showered," I remind him. "Let me cut your hair." My voice lacks conviction, and he knows it by the twinkle in his hooded eyes.

"I'll clean you—" His thumbs trace the fold under my chest. "Trust me." He winks.

Bending over, I cup his face and plant a kiss on his full lips. He opens his mouth, letting his tongue dance with mine. His hands leave my shirt and come to rest on my bottom again. He grabs both my cheeks firmly and a groan escapes his lips. My mouth explores his passionately, biting his lips when I can. Our saliva mixing makes me hotter, it's nothing like the wet dream from earlier. The fantasies in my head are running wild. I'd love to see him naked, taking me in front of his window for all to see—so close to the sun coming up, my chest on the glass, him pushing into me, and our fingers clasped—it'd be a breathtaking view for the neighbors.

"You keep trembling, Jade. Are you cold?" he mumbles between kisses.

I moan at his raspy voice, explicit and uncontrolled. "Just—*Fuck*, Aidan," I curse, my head dropping back, away from his touch. My aching body brings me back to reality. I wouldn't say no to a second round, but we just got back, and I haven't been this active with a man in a long time.

Aidan licks along my neck, sucking on my skin at several places, brushing his lips up and down, taking over my senses. "What were you saying?"

Breathing out calmly, I clear my mind and look at him. "I was thinking about you taking me in front of your window. But I don't think I can." I drop my gaze, feeling a pang of regret.

Slowly, he releases me. I've already memorized his smug smile. "Hey, don't make that face. It's fine." He winks. "How about I help you with the soreness?"

Suddenly, without any control on my part, Aidan lifts me onto the open window frame, resting my behind on the edge. I gasp but let him do what he wants. Hooking his fingers into my underwear, he pulls them down as I wiggle to help him strip me. The cool air hits my bare skin, intensifying my feelings. A tingling sensation tickles my outer lips and I tighten my stomach, anticipating the rest.

Aidan kneels in front of me, moving the stool back with his foot. His eyes dark with desire, he gently parts my legs while taking his time to caress my inner thighs. My breath hitches. "I can smell you," he whispers, biting his lower lips as if stopping himself from devouring me too fast. Moving his head forward, I get ready for his mouth on my legs, but it's his tongue that I feel. His breath is hot against my skin. Waves of pleasure make my body buckle and my hands grip the frame tightly to keep me from falling out the window. I keep myself from looking back—this man knows how to trigger my adrenaline, skillfully arouse my survival instincts and turn them into lust.

Leaving a trail of kisses up my flesh, he gradually approaches my pubic bone. With each brush, an electric shock hits me. Right in front of my cunt his nose tickles my hair causing my hands to grip the wood.

"Don't let me fall," I beg him, gasping for air, my eyes hooded.

He breathes out amusedly, nudging my core and the wetness dripping out of my hole. "You *will* fall, little driver," he promises with double-meaning. Aidan pauses, looks up at me with a playful glint in his eye.

I open my mouth to protest but he chooses this moment to press his lips against me, kissing me softly before his tongue flicks up and down to give me the friction I desperately need. My body arches toward him as he teaches me the lovers' language. The sensations are intense and I moan loudly, not caring for the outside world.

I almost bend backward to urge him closer to my most sensitive spot as he intensifies his movements, going deeper. My heart races with each swipe up my vulva. My breathing becomes ragged, my eyes flutter closed. I feel my control slipping away as pleasure builds fast. "Aidan," I plead without a single thought in mind, just to call his name as my body shakes.

My hand grips his hair, guiding him where I want. I fuck myself without limit, selfishly using him. I'm dripping all over the place, and I grunt louder in realization. His fingers slowly thrust inside of me while he begins to suck on my clit. Any past discomfort is swept away as I lose myself in his arms for the second time. My consciousness drifts momentarily, I know it to be the short moment that signals my climax. However, right before it happens, I notice a window opening above Aidan's apartment. It hardly matters and ignore it as he has me at his mercy.

"You taste so sweet," he murmurs, his voice muffled by his head buried between my legs. "Like it was made for me." My muscles tighten painfully around him, my grip on his strands pulls him closer as tension reaches its peak.

"More, more. Please—don't stop," I whimper, locking my body in place, clenching my jaw as my orgasm washes over me. Aidan guides me through it, increasing his pace and pressing his tongue flat against my soaked sex as I ride the wave. The explosion is as intense as earlier, especially since I've already been teased. Though, the euphoria disappears as quickly as it came.

Aidan gently soothes my sensitivity with a kiss, helping me come down from the high. He rises to his feet and, seeing me about to fall, quickly grabs my waist and guides me back inside. It's a miracle I haven't tipped over. And dying without panties would be downright humiliating.

I find I really enjoy his company, feeling more and more at ease the longer we spend together. Maybe it's the lack of close friendships in my life, or maybe it's the restless night I had, but in the end, I'm convinced it's because of Aidan's presence.

He hands me my underwear, beaming proudly, and I hurriedly put it on. "What?" I challenge him, struggling to maintain eye contact.

"I hope you're feeling less anxious now," he jokes, his lips still glistening with my release.

I burst out laughing, suddenly feeling a rush of relief. Indeed, it's an unexpectedly nice way to clear my head. After loosening my muscles, stiffened by our excitement, I'm able to organize my thoughts and decide to get back to what we were doing. "How about a fade instead of shaving it off completely?" I negotiate, knowing fully I'm incapable of doing it.

His eyebrows shoot up. "A *fade*? Weren't you the one scared to mess up?"

"Well, you can always shave it off," I remind him, mimicking his earlier tone.

He chuckles, clearly amused. Aidan is the kind of person everyone wants around. He's the reassuring voice, but also the one who calls for a time-out when things get too overwhelming. Maybe it's just an act, and he's normally the opposite of what he has shown me so far. But being with him calms my mind and gives my brain a break. Tonight, I'm going to make the most of it. Tomorrow, I'll start looking for a way to get my car running.

"You can do whatever you want. I'm not hard to please," he tells me, bearing the confidence for us both. I'd be terrified if I were him.

With a mischievous grin on my face, I stand up on my own, getting away from his reach and take the scissors we left on the bed behind. I walk with intentionally slow steps, toying with his trust. However, I realize pretty fast that Aidan *really* doesn't care.

"If I mess up, it's not *my* fault," I add, going around to position myself on his back.

Naturally, he pivots on the stool too, to look outside the window. "If you do, it's *entirely* your fault, Jade." Even his mocking remarks are lighthearted and harmless.

"You trust me with your hair, *so—*" I trail off, letting him come to terms with his future appearance. He must realize what I'm doing—dragging the thing to let him decide it's a bad idea. I'm a *driver,* not a damn hairstylist.

Silently, he exhales and raises his palm over his head to me. Understanding what he wants, I hand him the scissors and watch with utter horror as he grabs a few strands over his left ear and cuts to the roots. "There," he says, proud of himself, ignoring my agape mouth. "Now you have to cut so I don't look stupid. Can you do that?"

Shaking my head, I take the tool and start to cut from the back. The first snip is the most challenging, but the rest should go smoothly. I trim less than an inch of his length. Gradually, a calm atmosphere settles over the room. I'm not tired. If anything, I feel more energized than this morning. I'd like to think having a new friend helps, even though I might not meet that definition for him.

"What are you going to do with the Nissan?" he breaks the silence, but conversation isn't unwelcome.

I'll have to make extra efforts to pay for the repairs, but I'm not doubting myself. There hasn't been a moment in my life when I wasn't able to bounce back. The plan is simple: find a powerful car, abandon the idea of listing my profile on the application, and beg War for new jobs since the races are not on the table.

"Ask a kind mechanic to keep it in the garage until I get enough to pay for the damage?" I suggest sweetly, phrasing it as a question to avoid making it seem like I'm taking advantage of him for the favor.

"*Ah.*" Unintentionally, he swings his head backward, but I quickly protect him from the tip of the scissors by holding his head with my hand. "I wonder who that mechanic might be," he jests.

We can perfectly see each other in the now closed window ahead, but I still lean over his shoulder. He turns his head in my direction, and as our noses touch, I smile sweetly. "*Please*, Aidan. Will you keep my car until I get the money?"

He shrugs. "Okay," he agrees nonchalantly. I can hardly contain my excitement and immediately kiss him. He chortles when our lips touch, but accepts the gesture with a hum.

And here I was, thinking I'd have to call another tow truck to get it back to Greensburg. I'm relieved to have this weight off my shoulders, which means I can now relax and plan my next steps. It's going to be a bumpy ride. I trust Aidan not to rush me, he'll be patient. "It won't take long, just a couple of days, I promise. Thank you." I kiss his cheek. "*Thank you,*" I repeat when I straighten up.

"I'll take a look at it to see if I can do something."

"Please don't," I interrupt. Admitting I was the one who made the mistake was humiliating enough. Knowing he'll spot my error the moment he lifts the hood is plain terrifying. "You must have a lot of work. I don't want to bother you," I lie easily.

The black locks fall onto his back and chest, I brush them off to prevent any discomfort. I'll have to be focused when I do the fade, but for now, cutting suits me just fine. When I lift my gaze and meet his in the reflection, I realize that my attempt at appearing detached about the situation has failed miserably.

"You're not a bother, little driver." A pause. "What? Are you embarrassed?" he inquires, surprised. "You shouldn't be."

I follow the curve of his right ear as I trim around it, then blow on it to chase away the hair that has lodged there. "Your prices are too high," I confess, not saying anything about my lack of money.

He ignores the comment, and I can already anticipate what he's about to suggest next. "I can—"

"After we slept together? No, I won't accept any discounts."

Aidan's hilarity bursts out of him, and I have to take a step back to protect him from the tool again. "Oh, you can take advantage of me, Jade. You have my consent," he states enthusiastically.

"Stop that," I say without the intended animosity, yet horrified by the idea.

"What if I want to help you?"

I exhale deeply and lower my gaze when the weight of his becomes too much for me.

Aidan's help would be more than welcome, but I'm afraid of his opinion when he learns about the accident. A search of my name in the local newspaper would give him all the details. I've had time to accept the reputation the press has put on me. Most of what they said is not the entire truth of what happened, yet it still makes me a murderer. I *am* a murderer, but I'm not unredeemable.

Before I can think of a response, Aidan's attention shifts to his ringing phone, which he retrieves from his pocket. "Excuse me, I have to take this," he informs me.

"Sure. Do you want me to..." I motion to the bedroom door behind me with my thumb, asking if I should step out.

He quickly shakes his head, bringing the phone to his ear. "No, no. It's not that important."

As he greets the person and I do my best to give him privacy. I don't know why I reacted so reluctantly earlier, as I watch the haircut take shape, I realize it wasn't justified. It's not done—I still need to shave it and do the actual fade, but so far, keeping the length at the top was the best idea. Aidan is very attractive, and even bad hair wouldn't change that.

I put the scissors down and walk to the bathroom to retrieve the electric trimmer he left by the basin. When I come back, my distracted walk is halted by Aidan's intense gaze—undressing me unsubtly. Fully facing me, I stop in my tracks when I hear his next words.

"That's good, actually. I know the perfect driver for your race," he affirms, smirking mischievously.

CHAPTER 6

The Apocalys District in the City of Frost.

Million-dollar supercars sparkle under the lights, their presence is proof of the wealth of this city. Parked on the dirt, two hypercars stand out from the crowd. Priceless classic muscle machines lining before each other to find the perfect spot, their engines purring fiercely. Bikes—countless sports bikes—add to the music of revving engines. Frost's underground scene isn't just a show of power, it's America's own Monaco.

Being around these people feels surreal—a dream come true, even. It's been one of my biggest fantasies for as long as I can remember: seeing vehicles I've only ever dreamed of, mingling with people I've only watched from afar. They may be my age, but these individuals are *years* ahead of me, touching what I never will—abundance, endless possibilities.

But tonight is different. Tonight, *everyone* is on equal footing because that's what competition is all about. It doesn't care about someone's name or their past. What matters is talent, hunger for victory.

In the weeks that have passed, I've grown increasingly thankful for Aidan entering my life. After some tough negotiations, I finally allowed him to check my car and, no surprise, he found the issue—a turbocharger failure. Apparently, many people make the same rookie mistake I did. The mechanic told me he often saw this kind of problem in modified cars. With the popularity of JDM, he saw countless Supra, BRZ, and other Type R coming in with the same issues. He explained that the failure was not necessarily caused by my installation, but could be a mix of factors. Fixing the 240SX didn't give him too much trouble. He knows these cars better than I do.

So, Aidan and I made a deal. I wasn't sure what he would gain from it, but he claimed he wanted to help me. He agreed to fix my Nissan and gave me a credit, allowing me to pay it back little by little. But with the race he's already signed me up for, I hope to clear my debt once and for all.

In the past, the street races I've been to were organized last minute by an online group. The organizers would alert the drivers an hour before the start. it was rumored the bookie always tried to play us, so we often conducted bets on our own in secret.

Frost is an entirely different turf. Here, the races are a business, even a religion, for the masses ready to watch the spectacle on the half-finished Serpent Circuit. I've never driven on dirt before, and I'm seriously doubting Aidan's work on my Nissan. The last thing I want is to stall in the middle of a puddle and be stuck in front of the crowd. With hundreds of pairs of eyes here, having them all focused on me gives me the creeps. Yet he assured me it will hold on, and a part of me was gullible enough to trust him despite the signs.

Summoning my last bit of courage, I finally kill the engine at my designated spot on the starting line. Immediately, people gather around me and my opponents, but I pay no attention and quickly grab my jacket, opening my door.

Outside, the atmosphere is intense. The music blasts through mounted speakers, controlled by a DJ in the only standing building in this remote area outside of Frost. People dance, shout, sing, take pictures, and suddenly I'm transported back to my college years. Neon lights and lasers illuminate the area, and security guards are scattered around. If I didn't know better, I'd say I was attending an official racing competition, not an illegal street race. In Apocalys District, the black market thrives and bets are made with huge sums of money coming from hands that don't value these blocks of cash any more than a simple sandwich.

From the corner of my eye, I see some people inspecting every detail on my car. Some even chuckle when they see the mismatched panels. The different colors never bothered me—in fact, I think it brings a certain charm to the overall style.

"Yeah, it's an easy win for Billy. Look at *that*," one of them murmurs loudly enough for me to hear. The comment makes me smile to myself. People always underestimate what I have because of how it looks. A priceless car is useless for them to remember my name. I hope they bet on the wrong horses, I'll make more money in the end.

"Where are you from?" another one asks me.

I slam my door and lock it before facing him. I try not to let them shake my focus. "Greensburg," I answer flatly, looking around for Aidan, who promises to meet me here. Many '*ahs*' dances around me, all caring a double-meaning. Even if Frost's inhabitants have nothing to envy us, there's still this rivalry underneath. The one no one talks about because let's face it—our jealousy is understandable, *theirs* however can't be justified.

"I *knew* it would turn shit the moment Tearie replaced Caleb," another man jumps in.

Aidan gave me a rundown of the politics around here. The change in ownership that happened recently. Before Frost's races were snatched from its creator—Caleb—in Tearie's profit. He told me this person was an old friend of his he met at one of those races some years back. He didn't reveal much, except Tearie is only an alias. Obviously, the mystery having piqued my curiosity, I asked him about it, but he just laughed, saying that there weren't any words to describe Tearie, that I'd have to meet them.

A man, tall and broad, brings the attention of the small group to him. "Come on, let the outsiders join. It's cool to have more competition," he declares to the small gathering of reluctant faces. "Good luck," he sends my way with a wink, sipping on his beer bottle.

"Thanks," I grit through my teeth. As if reminded of the party happening further away, they all change in demeanor. It's too sudden that it has me turning on myself to look behind at the DJ, which seems to have captured their focus, only it's a woman I'm facing.

She looks at me under her nose, seemingly trying to decide how to address me. There's judgment in her eyes, but entertainment too. Entertainment, or is it playfulness? Slightly taller than me, I straighten up when her strange attitude raises my alarms. I'm not intimidated, but it's the second time I'm facing someone as commanding as War. I realize now the muscles, the gruffness, aren't what pushes me to obey, it's the *confidence*. More than that, it's a feeling of inferiority. I hate it, but it's not something I can change.

"You're Jade?" she asks curtly.

I frown at the unnecessary rudeness, or maybe it's only how she is and I'm misinterpreting everything. "Yes. You are?" I retort in a similar tone, though mine is a tad more condescending. I'm already getting ready to shield myself if she's another one of those Frost guys trying to mock me.

Slowly, a teasing smile spreads across her face, her eyes lighting up as she snorts. *Definitely making fun of me.* "Tearie," she says slowly, examining my reaction. And my embarrassment returns in full force.

I don't let anything show in my expression and pinch my lips hard, but she smiles knowingly. "Aidan said you were a good driver," she changes the subject, which I'm thankful for.

"I'm alright," I humbly reply.

She nods to herself, looking around and finding my car interesting as she takes a step toward it and bends forward to inspect my newly installed exhaust system from the back. From her position, she turns her head to show me she recognizes the expensive parts coming straight from a famous preparator. "I really like what you have here," she admits, impressed.

My shoulders slump in relief at having one of them praise me. The others, I couldn't care less about, but the Boss? Gaining a permanent ticket in her races might be possible if I make the right impression, which is exactly my intention.

Pushing aside the memory of our awkward first exchange, I stride to her side and point at the modifications Aidan has made, putting them on my tab. I choose not to say I currently lack the funds to repay him, allowing her to believe I can afford it. The last thing I need is for a wealthy woman to think I'm trying too hard to fit in—though fitting in is precisely what I'm aiming for.

"How long have you known Aidan?" My friend never mentioned coming here, even less knowing people living in the city of diamonds.

"We used to race for Caleb in Frost, but then he stopped coming. It's been a while since I've heard about him, but I needed fresh faces for tonight. He told me you'd be a great fit. It's nice to have a new driver around." Her friendly smile eases my nerves. I study her outfit for a moment—unlike everyone else, she chose combat boots and fitted black cargo pants. Her dark hoodie looks comfortable compared to the tight-fitting top I'm wearing. At first glance, a distracted eye could mistake her for a soldier, but focusing a second more on her face and her beautiful, soft features yet strong jawline would make anyone believe she's actually a model.

"Do you race too?" I look around at the other cars on the starting line, but I've seen the other racers earlier, and none of them were women.

"Not in cars, unfortunately." She laughs at a joke I don't get. The thought making her react in a way that has me thinking my question might have been ridiculous, had I known her. "I have work to do. I can't, actually," she explains, closing the matter. "Do you have the money?"

Another one of those rules Aidan warned me about—to participate in Tearie's races, you must pay. It's an entry fee fixed for all drivers. An expensive fee at that, which guarantees the exclusivity of Apocalys' races. *Apocalys* being the name of Tearie's business, if I remember correctly.

"Sure, let me get that," I inform her as I hurry to retrieve the sum in the glove compartment of my car. Back in front of her, I try to appear casual at handing her the five hundred dollars when I could use it to decrease my credit at War's garage. I'm not doubting this amount might be a simple lunch tab for her.

She simply puts the cash away in one of the many pockets of her pants, unafraid of being attacked by people who might want to steal it from her. Tearie trusts her power around here. Besides, she knows those people.

Taking out a tablet from her hoodie, she checks some bullet points and looks back up at me. "Can I have your driver's license, please?" she requires, looking bored over the procedures. It might be the first time an illegal business is this legitimate. If that's even a term I can use in this context. No wonder Apocalys is getting known outside of Frost.

Showing the small card, she takes a picture of it and scribbles some more on her device. I don't question what she's doing, I'd trust anything she tells me.

"We're good. Feel free to go around. Qualis starts at one." Pivoting on her side, she gestures to the only building with her thumb. "I think I saw Aidan inside. There's food and some equipment if you need anything. The top floor is for VIPs. If you want to get in, find Romana. The entry is two thousand for the year, all access. Only one night is one-forty. Questions?" she explains quickly.

Two thousand? To watch the races from a little above? It's baffling. "I'm good, thanks."

She smiles, looking me up and down. "Alright. Good luck. I'll be watching you, Jade," she says, giving me a wink before she turns around and leaves me here. Aidan was right—Tearie is not someone you can describe with words.

Finding myself all alone in the dark expanse of dirt that is the Serpent Circuit, I finally decide to join the mass of people. With thirty minutes to kill before the start, I push my way through the crowd to enter the building. Inside, no one would actually think we're at a street race, but more of a nightclub. I spot a couple of drivers laughing alongside some of their friends. I take the time to observe my opponents for the night.

First, there's the short man with leather gloves sipping on his water bottle. I saw him earlier getting out of his blue Corvette Stingray. Such a powerful machine would literally annihilate me on the circuit. If he already raced here, he has the advantage. He knows the curves, the layout. He'll be a challenge. Even if he's not that good, those details are enough to make a difference.

Second, we have the man dressed in a surprisingly formal attire for some unknown reason. I'm guessing he's the owner of the black and neon green BMW M4, considering he had a wrap all over the car with the number '54', the same number printed on his jacket. This man might be all show, but sometimes looks can also be deceiving. If his strategy is to have us underestimate him, it could work. Though the car is impressive, I noted he had it lowered. On a semi-dirt circuit, this does not bode well.

At the bar, a blond guy is talking to two women, trying to impress them. By his side, several empty shots are turned upside down on the counter. From my position, I can only see five, but I'm not sure how many of them the girls drank. This man was the one I was most worried about. Driving the McLaren P1, he seems confident enough in himself to indulge in alcohol before the race, even though, according to Tearie's rules, no drivers are allowed at the risk of disqualification.

Hands come around my body to squeeze my sides, interrupting my studying and tearing a jolt from me. "Jade," a voice whispers behind.

I jerk my head back and find Aidan grinning at me. "Where were you?" I ask, relieved to finally see someone familiar. The stress of the upcoming show is nearly enough to convince me I'll make a mistake and ridicule myself in front of everyone. Being alone in this kind of situation is mortifying.

His hands travel down until he rests them on my hips. Slightly bending forward, he presses a gentle kiss on my cheek. "Sorry, it's been a while since I've been here. Was catching up with some guys I know."

I look around at the many faces, my confidence crumbling progressively. "I'm not sure I can do it," I confess.

"What—hold on." Aidan catches my hand and drags me out, pushing through the many people to let us through the doors. I hear some grunting and curses thrown at him, but he doesn't care and continues to walk, clenching my hand tightly.

"Where are we going?" I ask at his back, but he doesn't answer. "Aidan," I call after him, trying to stop him in vain.

On the other side of the building, the sounds are faint. The noise is less overwhelming. Here, it's obvious Apocalys, and what Tearie does with the races, aren't simply for fun. It was hard to see it from inside, but the building is split in half—on one side, the party, the booze and music, but on the other, garages with a fully operational pit lane. The Serpent Circuit beyond the pits extends far away from us. The curves are clearly visible with the neon lights illuminating the track. It's bigger than I thought, going all the way to the forest limits at the far end of the district.

What is this place? What are those people? It can't be only a rich woman's crazy dream. What I've seen tonight reminds me of all the missions I've done for War. Tearie isn't simply a street race organizer, is she?

"The people you're racing with, Jade, I know them. They might have fancy engines, million-dollar cars, but none of them have the actual knowledge. Not like you do. They think they can race because they have a driver's license. Because they've only ever competed against one of their own, but I can assure you it doesn't take buying a sports car to know how to drive one." Aidan gently guides my gaze to his when I try to turn my head to the side.

I can feel his confidence, his trust in my abilities, yet there's still this part of me doubting. *Always* doubts. I am a driver—they are not. However, I still make mistakes sometimes. I shift too early or I tend to take the turns on the outside. Sometimes I forget about the dirty air when I'm racing.

Faced with my silence, Aidan sighs heavily. He then takes my head between his hands and presses his forehead to mine. His determination coursing through him until I can feel it in the warmth of his palms. "Look around, everyone is from Frost, aren't they?" he points out in a murmur.

I look at his piercing eyes. "Because it's incredibly expensive to race for Tearie," I answer flatly.

He snorts and moves his head back. "No. Because the rich kids are scared that outsiders might expose their lack of talent. Money can buy anything, but *not* victory."

"Even if I'm more talented than them, I don't stand a chance against a P1, Aidan. *Come on.* Let's be realistic for a second," I rasp, getting out of his hold. In front of me, he mirrors my gestures as I cross my arms over my chest, irritated.

"Oh, yeah. Your chances of winning are very low," he agrees, a playful expression dancing over his features.

I turn my eyes into slits and tilt my head, annoyed. "Your pep-talk was decent until now."

"*But,*" he says, raising a finger in the air. "Sometimes winning doesn't mean snatching the first place."

"What does that mean? Of course, it does."

"Show us what you're capable of. Show us how you handle pressure. That's the goal, Jade. Forget winning, give your best," he encourages enthusiastically.

"Us?" I prompt in response to the questionable expression on his face, enough for me to guess there's a double-meaning in his phrase.

"The spectators," he replies simply. "You're new here. Show them, little driver." He pecks my lips briefly before taking my hand once more. "Now come on," he says, leading me back toward the starting line.

It's the first time I'm dealing with a race format that's like nothing I've ever experienced before. Qualifications in street racing are unheard of for me, as the runs usually take place in urban areas, in the middle of traffic and under the threat of the police. But here, in the Apocalys District, it's different. The location is far enough from Frost to not attract attention, especially from authorities. This place is an illegal paradise for wild events, although strict rules are in place to maintain order. It's in everyone's interest to respect them.

Like all the other drivers, I've been isolated. Securely attached to my seat at the very end of the pit lane, I await my turn to enter the circuit and set a lap time. Tearie explained to us that each racer will have the circuit to themselves for five minutes—enough time for a formation lap and a timed lap. The latter will determine our place on the grid, with the quickest setting time securing the first spot and the slowest, the last.

As I wait for my turn, a million different thoughts flash through my head. I should observe the other drivers for my bet later, but I can't. "Jade, your turn," Tearie's voice echoes through the radio provided.

Engaging first gear, I guide the car onto the asphalt. Second gear, third. With increasing pressure on the throttle, I cross the pit lane exit, joining the circuit.

The sounds are muffled inside the car, cutting me off from the outside world. Utterly alone, I navigate the first turn, memorizing the curves. The formation lap allows me to drive at any speed within the five-minute limit, so I make the most of it, observing every detail. The neon lights on the ground make the track stand out. As for the bends, they're marked with fluorescent posts.

"You can do it. You can do it," I encourage myself, squeezing the wheel until my knuckles turn white. Approaching the challenging triple head-pin sector will undoubtedly be challenging at high-speed. The risk to be taken out or go out by myself is high. I'm hoping the drivers are not as aggressive as having death wishes.

Navigating each turn smoothly, I reach the starting line, its bright paint unmistakable.

This is it. Show them.

Without hesitation, I slam the throttle, shifting gears rapidly. My heart races, but there's no room for error now. I hope they're all watching because with adrenaline coursing through me, I'm confident in my abilities.

With laser focus, I cross the line, the timer ticking away.

racing the rich

CHAPTER 7

Apocalys District in Frost.

"I feel so humiliated," I complain to Aidan with my arms crossed and head bowed, kicking the dirt with my shoes as we approach Tearie to register my bet.

"Don't be. Qualifications are hardly a good example of what these cars will do when the race starts," Aidan reassures me, his good mood intact. "You're alone on the circuit, without anyone disturbing your time. Of course, the P1 will be first."

I snort. Aidan may have his secrets, but he certainly wouldn't abandon me in the middle of the action. I'm loving the way he takes care of me, like when he immediately wrapped his jacket around my shoulders after I parked the car because I was trembling like a leaf. The chemicals in my brain mistook my anxiety for a life-or-death situation. Aidan believes in me, and I can't let his enthusiasm go to waste just because I'm doubtful.

Slowly reaching for his head, I stroke the side of it, brushing his black hair back from his face. While I did my best cutting it, I had to give up and ask him to visit a hairdresser to fix my failed attempt at shaving the edges straight. Now, more handsome than ever, Aidan made me promise I'd continue to cut his hair if he ever needs it. I agreed, knowing I can only improve with time, and it's also a good way to spend time together.

"Thank you," I mouth silently, showing my gratefulness through my eyes.

Bending over me, locking us into our little bubble surrounded by the crowd, he gently kisses my nose, which causes me to rise on my tiptoes to properly have his mouth on mine. But my lips accidentally meet his teeth, yet it hardly matters as he deepens our embrace and caresses my hair affectionately.

Worried we're getting too carried away, we simultaneously step away from each other. Though, the playfulness in our gaze promises to find the other again after the race, whether for comfort or celebration.

"The bet," he reminds me.

"The bet," I acknowledge with a nod, shaking off the neediness. For now.

With a smirk, he takes my hand and guides me to the board where Tearie has listed the odds, minimum bet, driver standings, and other race details.

My name, assigned number for the night, grid position, lap time, and odds for winning the race are all displayed: Jade, 29, fourth, 1"53, 10:1. I glance at the others, unsurprised by the results. With a ratio of 2:1, the McLaren is obviously the favorite for the first place. The Corvette for the second, and the M4 for the third. I'm closing the grid with a thirty-seven-second difference from the BMW. As I said: *humiliating.*

"Don't make that face, little driver, at least your bet shouldn't be that difficult to make," Aidan murmurs only for me to hear as we stop in front of the bookie with her tablet. Beside her stands another woman, shorter, with a beautiful dress and a half-up, half-down hairstyle that perfectly complements her face. With her full lips and soft features, she's as beautiful as Tearie, but in a more conventional way.

"How'd you like the Serpent, Jade?" Tearie asks, raising an eyebrow.

"Curvy," I reply without emotion.

She chuckles while the woman by her side takes a step forward. "Told you. Luxuria went too far with the sketches. We should have listened to Fyra. At least we would have had more straights," she complains in a sweet voice to Tearie.

But Tearie only shrugs and addresses me once again. "Jade, Aidan, this is Romana, my colleague," she introduces us, pointing her finger at the woman. Romana doesn't seem to like that title, crossing her arms and frowning.

"*Tearie,*" she calls out, injecting as much animosity as she can into her name.

While the race organizer teasingly sends her a kiss in the air, Aidan replies for the both of us, "Nice to meet you."

"Can I bet on anything?" I ask Tearie, curious about the flexibility of her rules.

"Pretty much," she agrees. "I can create odds on anything you ask. Though the others usually put their money on who's going to win."

"I don't want to do that," I tell her. The existing odds are not interesting enough for me. Betting on my win would be the worst mistake since I have zero chance of winning, so I'll have to play it smart. What is interesting enough for me to have my attention on is my ratio. My results are terrible enough for the others to not even consider adding me to their bets. The fewer people betting on me, the greater the odds. "*Me*, not finishing last," I announce confidently.

Tearie looks around in thought, doing the math in her head. When an idea crosses her mind, she disappears behind her tablet and scribbles what I imagine are possibilities and scenarios to ensure *the house wins*. My stare finds Romana's, and she stops her scrutinizing to friendly smile at me. I match her expression. It's refreshing to be the stranger around here. No one knows me, which means I can be whoever I want.

"Ratio nine-to-one. Minimum is two-hundred," Tearie finally declares.

So, for every dollar bet, there's possibly a nine-dollar win. Betting the minimum and winning the bet would mean *one-thousand and eight hundred dollars*. But, written at the bottom of the board are Apocalys' vigorish—twenty percent. With the commission deducted from the total payout, that would actually mean a bag of one-thousand, four-hundred and forty dollars, plus the original bet amount.

One-thousand, six hundred and forty dollars. That is if I bet *only* two-hundred dollars.

I glance at Aidan on my side, biting his lips to hide the smile trying to break through. He trusts my skills. He trusts my driving and the car he spent hours modifying with the most expensive black market add-ons. I can't let him down, and for that, I need to be as confident as he is.

Facing Tearie again, I give her my best smile and reach for the inside of my skirt, where I hid the cash against my belly. When I hand her the money, she counts it in front of our watchful eyes. I don't have a single dollar left, my bank account is dry, and I'm going to be in a lot of trouble if I don't win this bet. *Damn it, what am I doing?*

"Three hundred and twenty-two dollars. You have a *lot* of nerves. I know someone who'd love to meet you," she giggles as she glances at her friend, harboring a similar reaction.

I ignore their closeness and turn away. Aidan trailing behind me, I get out and find the music blasting a little louder than before, the atmospheric are waiting for the show. They want an exciting race. They don't care about who will win and who will not, what they're after is the *spectacle*. The electricity in the air makes the hairs on my arms raise, my breathing quickens, and a grin curls the corner of my lips.

"You certainly made a statement back there." Aidan's laughter fills the air as he seizes my hand and twirls me around like a ballerina on the dusty ground.

"Do you think she'll remember me?" I shout over the loud bass, my face frozen in a beaming expression.

"Jade, I'd bet everyone here will," he confirms, giving me a pointed look.

Suddenly, a shrill buzzer goes off simultaneously as a red countdown is displayed on a LED board by the building's entrance. On it, a clock counting in reverse from five minutes. At its sight, the people scream, the music changes, accelerating our heartbeats to an impossible speed. Others run to the cars, tapping on them rhythmically, even on my 240SX. Girls circle around some drivers while they send competitive looks at each other. I'm left absorbing the energy on my own, deciding whether I should find some calm before to gather my thoughts or take part in this insane pre-race ritual.

Aidan makes the decision for me by dragging me to my car, positioned in fourth place on the grid. In front of me is the Corvette, and by my side the M4.

"Good luck, outsider!" a man shouts at me. Following his cheers, multiple others do the same. Normally, I'd feel embarrassed by the attention, but the night fell a while ago, and the neon lights cast a new look on the many faces. I can be whoever I want—the driver, the outsider competing in the exclusive street race in Apocalys District. The girl with *nerves*.

So I wink at them, nodding to accept their encouragement. In front of everyone, Aidan lifts me and sets me on my black hood. As if I've already learned the gesture, my muscles act on their own, and I immediately wrap my legs around him, pulling his body close to mine and securing him with my arms around his neck. Both smiling childishly at the other, I taste his lips. He takes his time exploring my mouth again, biting me, which makes some whimpers erupt from my throat. Little sounds only he can hear.

My right hand grips his locks while the other draws circles on his nape. Contrary to his habits of placing his under my shirt, he only grabs my waist to maintain my body in place while his tongue runs on my teeth. His presence makes me warm all over, and I'm becoming excited about something else than the race at this moment.

My body responds to his as if we have our own private language. The people around haven't stopped screaming and dancing, building the race start with a strong atmosphere no one can escape. If I could, I would spend eternity in this place, feeling this way, sharing my restlessness with him. I know he lives for the present, just like I do. None of us would trade it for anything. It's one of the reasons I can't see myself growing old—the races, the adrenaline, my car—it's only temporary. There'll be a time when I'll have to put the keys back, but that time hasn't come yet. There're many races I have yet to take part in and countless circuits my car has yet to master.

With Aidan by my side, I'll eventually dominate those nights, make a name for myself no one will ever forget.

My chest presses against his, and the curve of my back allows him to crash his pelvis into mine. With his body almost lying on mine, we lose track of time, lose ourselves in the other. I might be intoxicated by him, by the power his mouth has on mine, but it's not something I'd ever fight against. In our bubble, I smile because I found someone who might actually stay by my side, even if I confess about my past. He might stay despite my insecurities and my anxiety. He might stay even if I push him away.

"It's time," I murmur against his skin, softly breathing his air.

As if drunk by our kiss, Aidan opens his eyes with difficulty. The desire is palpable, matching what I feel for him. He hums, agreeing, and kisses me once again, this time with his eyes open.

I'll happily follow him wherever he wants to take me. I care very little for the people around. There's only Aidan in my eyes, and I hope I will not disappoint him, because I have no wish to have him as a consolation prize.

The little voice at the back of my head reminds me of a curious thought that occurred some days ago when he pulls back from me, brushing a wild strand of hair behind my ear. This man—with countless tattoos, manager of the garage owned by someone no one wishes to cross paths with—knows more about the street races in the region than I do. *This* man jumped head first to help me fix my car, happily opened a tab at the garage when I couldn't afford it. The mechanic who has incredible driving skills. Someone War would trust enough to—

"You're—" I begin, but cut myself off before I ask him what's really on my mind. I need to know more about his motives. Why is he doing all of that? It can't be because he likes me, that's not a reason to equip the Nissan with priceless mods.

"Thirty! Twenty-nine!" the crowd loudly cheers, counting down to the start.

"You're alright?" Aidan asks, mistaking my expression for nervousness.

"Yeah," I answer, still frowning at the obvious signs right in front of me, yet I bluntly ignored from the beginning. As I jumps off the hood, I look at him once more, hiding any emotions in my features to only show my determination. "I have to get ready. See you after."

"I'll be in the VIP section, watching you from above," he promises. "You'll do great, Jade."

I ignore him and settle behind the wheel. Fastening my harness, I watch as guards guide the mass away from the circuit. All alone with the three men, each of us in our respective car. I grip the steering wheel at nine and three, focusing my gaze on the front, not planning to look elsewhere.

The music has stopped, now only the vibration of the engines can be heard. I exhale, chasing out of my lungs the remnants of tenseness from earlier.

The ambiance shifts quickly, the airflow stops, and all thoughts evaporate.

In front of us, a woman appears, waving a flag. She points at the McLaren driver in the first place with her perfectly manicured index finger. "Ready?" She must scream, but her voice is easily muffled by the roar of the powerful machines all around her. She does the same with the second and third, before her gaze finds mine. "Ready?" she mouths at me, and in response, I make my 240SX purr with a single rev.

The present stops for a second. Immobile, she builds the chase's excitement like a deer letting its fur be seen outside the bushes for the wolves to see.

I don't dare move, not even breathe.

In one motion, she lowers the flag.

The night race begins with the roar of the loudest—the sleek P1 leads the pack with an impressive acceleration. The rest of us are left with the dust flying in its rear. Second on the grid, the blue Stingray uses its V8 fully, following the orange tornado. The black and neon green M4 has no problem keeping up with the pace, finding the right balance between speed and skills.

Despite my heavy mods, I'm off to a slow start compared to the others. I know I'll have to use more strategy than power if I want to give them a run for their money.

The first corner is quite difficult for everyone. Ahead of me, I can see the M4 going out on the left, bringing more dirt and gravel onto the circuit.

Knowing my weaknesses, I don't take the turns like the others do. After all, it's not what I'm known for in Greensburg. Though I had to find a compromise—drifting and racing are, after all, very different activities. For that exact reason, I installed medium compound tires for better grip. This circuit is tricky because of its nature. It wouldn't be impossible to slide over the turns, but I'm afraid of losing control if I even try to do it here.

I hit the apex sooner than most, choosing a driving line slightly to the right compared to the car in front, but so far, it works well. Thanks to this technique,

I avoid the cloud coming out of the BMW and can come at rear-level with him.

Tearie said there were rules during the race—though crashing an adversary on purpose isn't against the rules for some reason. Keeping that in mind, I'm forced to brake sooner than the man before me and steer the car off course when we enter a bend. I don't know these guys and how they'll react if they lose.

My mouth hurts from clenching my jaw, and my frustrated groans become louder than the rumble of the engines. Despite the distraction, I fight to maintain my focus, my tunnel vision unwavering. Yet, even I find it difficult not to be impressed by the P1 far ahead. The race leader has superior...*everything*, not even the Corvette seems to be a worthy competitor. Though, on the straights, the raw power of the blue car shows its real strength and manages to keep him close. His struggle on the corners is easily forgotten.

The few high-speed sections aren't an advantage for the Stingray only—both the M4 and I close the distance. I don't know these guys, but one thing is sure: they drive expertly and I'm slightly bitter I underestimated them. The black car even *fights* against the Corvette for second place.

The twists and curves never end on the Serpent, and none of us are able to stay on the track going this fast. The Stingray even cuts one corner, bringing the car by the McLaren's side. But that fight isn't mine, especially not when I have the rear of the M4 right in front of my eyes. I scream victory because it's time for the triple head-pin section, where the talent of the driver is everything.

Instantly, upon taking the first chicane, the orange beast goes off-track, letting the Corvette take the lead temporarily. Until the raw power of his car betrays him and sends him out, too. The P1 becomes the head again, in time for the M4 to engage in the first corner, and I, right behind. I note as the car in front struggles at maintaining it on track and take the turn simultaneously.

"My chance," I grumble with eagerness.

The Corvette is decided to *not* be talented at all and give up trying to properly take the pins. As a result, the M4 passes the Stingray and me right behind. When the guy zig-zags in front of me and takes the last pin a little too on the outside, I take the opening and pass him on the inside. Obviously, he closes the corner sooner in hopes of blocking my move, resulting in the both of us going off-track while the Corvette passes us, taking the second place *once again.*

"*Fuck! Fucking* ass—You little *bitch!*" I scream at the top of my lungs, hitting the steering wheel, not being able to control my rage. Through my window, I scowl at him, to which he responds by showing me his middle finger. I ignore him and focus back on my race, bringing my car back on track several precious seconds before him. Now third, I know I can't make other mistakes if I want to win my bet.

The second lap has begun, the M4 is still behind me and seems to have a hard time closing the gap between our two cars since the crash. From the start, I knew this section would be challenging for all of us, but after successfully taking advantage of it, a newfound motivation pulses through my veins. I had little to no optimism earlier but now, delusion took hold of me, and I can even see myself winning this.

It's wishful thinking, but surprisingly, it helps. I'm more in line with my car. I can feel the dirt under my wheels, the wind caressing the curves of my 240SX. The engine sends vibration in my thighs, and the artificial lights reflect on the roof. I flawlessly navigate the triple head-pin for a second time without veering off-course. I take the curves properly, hit the apex at the right time, and catch up with the Corvette when I'm out of it. Everyone loses time in that part, but not *me*. Not anymore.

On the third lap, I come very close to the Stingray, but it seems to be never enough to pass it. It doesn't bother me that much because if I maintain my pace, I'm certain I'll make it out third, as hoped.

The fifth and last lap—the final stretch. The current grid hasn't changed, yet the M4 came close last tour. However, a quick trip to the triple-head and it's back at its place, last and behind me. I'm doubting the driver's mentality at this moment—fearing he might retire or resort to a reckless maneuver to avoid finishing last on the Serpent. This would mean I'd take the humiliating place and lose my bet. Even though he's clearly irritated, he stays in the race. I just hope he holds on until we all cross the finish line.

The Corvette becomes a tough fighter. I'm not a threat to him since I don't have the car for it. Which is why I don't get why he's protecting his position so aggressively. But it's still a race, and people are here for the show, so I join in this ridiculous battle and try to pressure him from behind. I brake later than usual in some corners and make him believe I'll go for it. My bumper tickles his rear once, which he doesn't seem to appreciate very much by the violent steering to the left, cutting short my next turn.

Far ahead, the woman from the start is back, but now she's on the side of the road. The P1, without a doubt, affirms its supremacy and maintains the lead toward the end. It speeds one last time and crosses the line, taking the victory with an overwhelming lead over us.

As we approach the last straight, the Corvette struggles to maintain control, skidding off-track onto the dirt. The gap between us closes rapidly, and my heart pounds in my chest.

I floor the throttle, urging my car to give everything it has. A desperate cry escapes my lips, I pray it can last just a few more seconds. The Stingray and I surge forward *side by side*. He must be watching me, but my gaze remains fixed ahead, focused on the finish line. One last stretch. *One last stretch.*

Pedal to the metal, I hold my breath. The engine roars louder. As we cross simultaneously, the air is thick with the suspense. *Who* is second?

The race ends when the BMW joins us in the pit lane. Spectators hurry all around us, smiling, screaming, with alcohol already pouring.

I win my bet, no matter the end results, I did it.
I did it!

The people circle around the winner, but the same mass can be found around each driver, me included. There are many congratulations and praises.

I jump on my hood and pump my fist in the air, causing them to create havoc all over. The winner quickly brings back the attention to him, but it hardly matters when I spot Aidan among the bodies, grinning from ear to ear.

"Aidan!" I exclaim, my arms widespread and bending on my knees to silently ask for him to help me down.

He hurries, his hands already around my waist, right before I throw myself into his arms. "You did it! I knew you would,"—he kisses my face repeatedly—"you're amazing, Jade," he adds, pampering my cheeks with his contagious affection. "Fuck. That was insane. Watching is..." At a loss for words, he shakes his head, closing his eyes while still holding me close. Full of adrenaline still, I crash my lips to his. I don't waste any time and almost indecently devour him right here, which makes him giggle against my lips.

"I won the bet," I happily announce.

When he finally lets me down, it's to cup my face and kiss my nose. "I think you're ready," he says.

Frowning, I grip his shirt to keep him close when the people around try to pry me away from him to join the podium on the side where Tearie undoubtedly awaits with the results. "Ready for what?"

Aidan winks and brushes my hair around my ear, letting his thumb linger on my lobe. "I'll tell you everything when we get out of here."

I was certain he hid something from me. Though I don't have it in me to be angry at him, not when I know I have my place on the podium. Second or third, I'm about to figure it out.

what are you hiding?

CHAPTER 8

In Frost.

The chemicals in my brain are still highly active, my blood burns, forcing me to turn on the air conditioner in the car. I can't help it—my eyes glance at the passenger seat every other second to make sure the money is still there in my bag. I have to feel the paper and see if I can count the cash just by touch.

I haven't stopped smiling. Tearie had to make a choice—the Corvette or the Nissan? Allow the outsider to challenge the sports cars of Frost or play it safe and reassure her contacts. She's the most unexpected woman I've met in the street racing community. A woman full of power but likes the taste of chaos. Knowing that, it's natural she chose me. And with the second-place title at the exclusive Apocalys race, the people are already waiting for my comeback.

My cheeks hurt, but what can I do? I have a lot more money than anticipated, the organizer's number on my phone, and Aidan driving in front of me. I control the rush of emotion but when I see the brake lights on his RX-7, my muscles lock up with nervousness.

He said I was *ready*, which is an unsettling phrase that piques my curiosity. Tonight, I'll finally find out if my guesses are right or wrong. As I said, the signs are there, open for me to guess.

Slowly, the Mazda turns into what appears to be an opening leading to nowhere. A clean gravel path between the trees, guiding us into the dense forest. I'm not afraid of the night, but the lack of moonlight, of *life*, worries me.

Aidan thinks I'm ready, I remind myself. Surely, he's not about to reveal murderous tendencies.

The road ends in a vast parking area. The setting is faithful to the image we have of Frost Forest: neat, even if this part of the city is far enough away from everything to be overlooked.

I park next to him and wait until he gets out of his car before I do. But only after tucking the money under my seat in case someone sees it. "Are you going to kill me?" I question, laughing nervously while glancing around for any signs of life. It's *only* him and me.

"*Jade*," he exhales, brushing the comment off as ridiculous. "You know why I brought you to a secluded place," he murmurs, stepping in my direction. The double-meaning is clear on his face—hooded eyes, a slight smirk, and slumped shoulders. The strands of hair falling on his forehead give him this look I find myself hard to resist. I watch him, and he is everything I ever wished for. Aidan's my friend, there're no doubts, perhaps even more.

A few inches away from me, the mechanic hides his hands in his jeans pockets to keep from touching me, as the discussion we're about to have seems rather serious. I'm torn between enjoying the win with him as we wanted, and risking the bond that's shyly forming between us.

But I reason with myself and push away the deep attraction I have for him. "What are you hiding?" I start, inviting him to talk.

His reaction comes fast—he seems to think over his next words carefully. Moistening his lips and avoiding my gaze to look at the sky in wonder. "Something you need to know before we continue. But..." He pinches his lips tightly and clenches his jaw while lowering his head. "I don't want you to think I used you. It's never been my intention," he claims, his eyes fixed on mine.

Used me? Does he mean sleeping together? I have nothing of value to give him, if that's the case. Nothing to offer. There has to be another reason. All at once, the possibilities I wanted to forget but couldn't assail me. He was ready to help modify my car with improvements I could never afford; he gave me enough of his story to feel for him... Was he manipulating me? Playing with me?

"You're such a liar, Aidan," I spit, finally accepting the truth and coming to terms with my fate.

"You pretended to be my friend because you're the one I'm fighting against, aren't you?" my voice cracks. My vision, turning blurry, prompts me to look elsewhere. But not before I witnessed the pity look written all over him. I stare at my feet when I say the next words, not keen on seeing his reaction. "You're War's driver, aren't you?" I can't help it, I quickly glimpse at his face when he nods and drops his head back to grip at his hair.

"You need to understand—"

"*What*? That you've been playing with me from the start? Did you find it funny to see me struggle in front of him, knowing I had no chance because he would pick *you*?" I rasp, not in anger but in *hurt*. I don't feel betrayed, but I genuinely thought I had found a friend who understood what it's like to work until exhaustion to be noticed by the right people. Money always comes first, but having a chance to impress someone like War means so much more.

"Jade, no. There are other things that you don't know," he tries, raising his hands, attempting to calm me. In vain, my racing thoughts ache in my brain already. This, mixed with the aftermath of the competition, is a deadly combination for my health.

"It was just a twisted game for you." My head shakes rapidly, trying and failing to make the tears disappear. I want to scream, but more than anything, I want to never have met him in the first place.

"I was testing you," he declares firmly, dropping the biggest piece of information, the last of his secret. But scratching his head shows me that's not how he wanted to reveal it. I watch motionless, waiting for the rest, when he crosses his arms over his chest and bites his lips. He puffs, lets out a word of encouragement to himself, and paces in front of me. "War told me about you. Asked me to keep an eye on you. It was long ago." He gestures in the air to emphasize this distant time. "He thinks you're good, so I wanted to see it for myself."

"You were *spying* on me?" I accuse, dumbfounded.

He tilts his head to give me a moment to think it over. War is powerful because he knows everything about everyone. I knew he had my life in one of his files.

"No, I didn't," he states, and I believe him. Everyone has a role—a driver isn't a spy. "I've been to one of your races in Greensburg. It was a while ago. You need to know that you're the only one he allows in the garage, Jade. The *only* one that isn't from the circle."

"I've proved myself to him. Of course, he trusts me with some jobs," I remind him. I have assets none of them have: I'm from Greensburg; I've known this city all my life, which makes me an invaluable pawn against the ones War considers his enemies.

Aidan stops his nervous walking and tries to come close to me, but I step back until the side of my car blocks any more retreat.

"War's very strict with people he trusts. Some missions are not for everyone. But you've been allowed to know some of his motives, and I think it speaks volumes."

"Then why bother testing me? I know who he's hiding from. I've heard the rumors. That's why he keeps me around, right?" I look for reassurance, but I'm met with the same expression.

"You're an exceptional driver, and yes, you've shown you can handle the jobs. But it wasn't enough for War. He wanted you around, but eventually his paranoia won, and he looked for ways to cut ties with you. To only give the missions to the circle," he reveals slowly, as if he's sorry it had to happen. I understand better why I had so much trouble reaching the boss. All of this comes down to one name: Maddox Ryder. Finally, I'm feeling *used*, like he mentioned.

"I'm not valuable enough, and I'm clearly not part of the circle. It looks a lot like a game to me, Aidan," I accuse sarcastically. My stare is murderous, yet I still control my emotions until the end.

Aidan hisses, knowing how everything looks from my perspective. I'm convinced he screwed my chances. Maybe it was a team effort, and the circle did everything to keep me out. They eventually succeeded.

"I *saw* you. I *watched* you. Trust me when I say you deserve the spot," he assures me. Eyebrows furrowing, I question him silently. So, he clarifies. "I'm not the only driver in War's inner circle. There are three of us. Over the years, War recruited us. Most stayed, others met their fate," he finishes in a small voice.

Immediately, our discussion when I was cutting his hair pops into my head. The tattoos, the promises. "Death or prison," I murmur.

He nods, confirming. "War trusts me. *Me* and the others. When I told them you were perfect to replace Noah, they reacted badly. The boss already didn't want to contact you. Maddox Ryder is getting closer to our location by the day. It's getting risky to allow..." He holds the last word from getting out of his mouth, but I understand perfectly what he's trying to say. I've been hearing this word all evening: the *outsider*. He takes a deep breath and resumes, "But I'm convinced you're the right choice. For that, I had to make a deal with them. I'm sorry, Jade, but they wouldn't have given you a chance otherwise."

He didn't tell me anything to protect the group, including the boss. I'm the hazard, the piece of the puzzle that can't be controlled. In their minds, I'm either the weak link, or the one they need.

"What if I don't want it? What if working for War wasn't what I wanted to do anymore?" I blurt out. He had no right to assume anything about my intentions. I *want* to work for War—it scares me, and I'm pretty sure it will forever—but I would've appreciated it if someone had asked for my opinion.

What I have been dreading has finally come, and the choice to back up and not involve myself in dangerous businesses is no longer available. With the test and the spot available in the inner circle, my future is right in front of me.

I can still refuse everything, but I know too much already. What if War sends someone my way to make sure I never open my mouth? What if, five years from now, I find a job as a driver and realize I made a terrible mistake because I'm still struggling to pay rent, buy groceries, and have no cash for emergencies?

"I'd think that's a shame, but it's your choice. With what you did tonight, Jade, that's all it takes to convince them," he argues. I'm not sure what prompts him to come closer, but he does. The tip of his sneakers touches my shoes, but other than that, he doesn't try to initiate contact.

"They're doubting my skills?" I'm surprised. If anything, that should have been the one thing about me they could trust, no questions asked.

"No, only your competitiveness, how you control your emotions. A driver isn't good just because they know how to drive, but because they know what it takes to finish a race," he reminds me, curling up his lips to show me he's joking.

"You're ridiculous, Aidan," I breathe out, rolling my eyes. Looking at his arms, I'm tempted to trace the ink with my finger. Instead, I push him back by moving to the front of the cars. Observing the empty parking lot, I smile at the stars that aren't visible enough in the city. It's a shame the most perfect time of the night would be wasted with light pollution.

It's night, dark and reassuring. Like always, I feel the need to enjoy this moment with everything I have. Even in a place I don't know, with a man who lied to me, those are reasons that aren't strong enough for me to shake the feeling away.

As I walk toward the tree line where the trail into the forest begins, I hear the faint sounds of his steps following me. I ignore him when I wander without purpose.

"There's something else," he breaks the silence after some minutes of hiking. I'm not annoyed by it, his voice is low enough to not cover the sounds of nature.

I stay on the trail, following it, and glance back to catch him already watching me. This time, there's no pity or anxious contortion of his face. Aidan is back to being the playful and never-bothered guy I've known for the past few weeks.

"What?" I snort. "Is Tearie involved too? *Oh, wait,* is the woman at the Balkans club actually War's girlfriend, and he was *also* testing me then?" I sarcastically guess, a mocking smile directed at him. I've had enough of secret revelations for tonight.

Naturally, the mechanic chortles at my attempt to be angry with him. In two strides, he's in front of me, his hands on my waist to stop me from moving past him. My gaze is fixed on his face while he scrutinizes my every feature—my lips, my nose, my neck.

"You're not the only one we're testing. You're *one* of the candidates we're considering for the driver's spot," he announces.

CHAPTER 9

In Frost Forest.

Torn between cursing his entire family tree and turning around to leave this madness behind, I narrow my eyes angrily. "Are you kidding me?" My shoulders slump, frustration creeps up my spine. Not only am I not taken seriously and almost discarded completely by the boss, but now they've put me in a competition against others without my permission.

"If it was up to me, you'd be the one to join us, but the others also have their preferences. War included," he says

"So, I'm not the first choice." I look at his face and see his lips pressed together. "The second?" Slowly, the muscles of his mouth relax to let a slight twitch through. My eyes widen. "The *third*?" Aidan fully grins now.

"You're unbelievable." I grip his wrist to release his hold on me and swiftly take a step back to leave. But, I'm suddenly stopped in my tracks when I'm lifted off the ground. His arms, a firm lock over my ribcage, prevent any escape. I wiggle, but Aidan only tightens his embrace.

"Put me down," I order firmly.

He laughs and kisses my cheek. "You'll make it. Wait until I tell them about tonight," he reassures me, but I'm not sure I trust anything coming out of his mouth anymore.

"Aidan, I'm not laughing." He lowers my body until my feet rest on the ground but never lets me go. Instead, one of his arms reaches for my belly under my top. "*Aidan,*" I warn through gritted teeth.

"Yes?" he murmurs in the shell of my ear. His warm breath caresses the delicate skin of my nape until he presses his soft lips to the curve.

A long, breathy exhale escapes my lungs as I try to focus on what he makes me feel rather than bitterness. "Don't you dare," I threaten again, yet this time, it's more of a plea. One lacking much conviction. "*Don't.*"

He opens his mouth and lets his tongue flick out, tempting me. I've completely stopped moving. He drops a kiss, then another. "Or what?" he playfully remarks.

I could tell him I'd easily overpower him, it shouldn't be that difficult. Damn him, because I want to shut my mouth and see what he'll do next. And the wait is short when he abruptly and unexpectedly bites my neck. I yelp in surprise and try to jiggle out of his arms, but he clutches my body. His palm has flattened on my stomach, his thumbs playing with my sanity while his mouth starts to suck.

"What are you doing? I'm going to mark," I whimper, slumping against his torso.

The seconds pass, and progressively, the pain of having my neck brutalized turns into a warm sensation spreading to my heart. A tingle barely aching anymore. I let him do what he wants, savoring the night in the process. The leaves dancing with the wind, the occasional animal running around us, adds to the overall experience.

Inhaling with difficulty, I let out a small squeak he ignores. When he finally leaves my skin, my eyes flutter shut. He gently kisses the wound that will undoubtedly fade into a rosy shade in a couple of hours. "Trust me," he whispers between brushes of his nose on my face.

Still pressed against him, I raise my hand to touch the tender part of my neck. He blocks my attempt by pecking my fingers to distract me, which stupidly makes a giggle erupt from my throat.

"*Oh? She laughs?*" he cheerfully notes.

I try to bottle up the sounds as best I can, just to spite him, but what I've been dreading happens when his hand inside my shirt starts to tickle my side. My attempts to cover up any noise are reduced to nothing—I burst out laughing in his arms. Wiggling, thrashing, and trying to kick his legs behind, Aidan doesn't let me breathe for a second. He follows my hilarity and nearly undresses me when he tries to catch me falling to my knees.

"Stop! Stop! Stop!" I beg when enough air reaches my lungs.

He doesn't listen. He hovers over me and cackles when I scream. Only then does he stop. Chuckling still, he takes his hands off me. Out of breath and unexpectedly tired, I lay on the ground to catch up. Watching the stars and gulping air with my mouth agape.

Aidan sits on his haunches beside me, looking delighted. "Are you mad at me, little driver?"

"You're childish."

Smirking and squinting, he reaches for my hair to brush them back—on the dirt, apparently. "Am I?" he taunts as he places his hands on either side of my head to give him enough support to swing a leg over me and sit astride my belly.

I snort, looking around to ensure no one's nearby. My body is utterly calm, entirely fascinated by the man over me, bringing his face impossibly close to mine. "You should've never hidden something like that from me," I criticize him. He should've come to me and told me face-to-face. Maybe, I would've accepted to play.

"I'm sorry. I promise there's nothing else you don't know. I wanted to make sure you were right for us. The stakes are so high we hardly have any margin for error," he explains, apologetically.

Nodding, I lift my arms and encircle his neck to pull him to me. His lips, aligned with me, press gently against mine for a brief moment. "I don't know what made you believe I stand a chance against other pros. I've never done anything like it," I complain, lacking the confidence I had on the Serpent.

"I don't know what makes you believe you don't. You drive and you fight until there are no more doubts. Like I said: to me, the spot is yours," he affirms.

Strangely, it's all it takes to relax me for the time being. He trusts my skills, why shouldn't I? Of course, it's easier said than done, and the moment I meet the ones I'm competing against, I'll welcome back the anxiety and nervousness, but for tonight, I'm alright.

"Does that mean you'll stop spying on me now?" I tease.

"I didn't," he firmly states.

Giggling, I rock my hips from left to right, trying to find room between his legs to move freely. "Whatever you say. *Liar*," I sing-song. However, my joke ends abruptly when, with his right fist, he grabs both my wrists and slams them to the ground above my head. That effectively shuts me up. My heart pumps harder, and I'm mesmerized by the reflections of the moonshine on his black hair. The locks, a curtain around his face, give his stare the darkest shade. He moistens his full lips, all the while staring at mine in hunger. But what arouses me the most is the delicate silver chain necklace about to fall out of his shirt.

Aidan kisses my forehead, bringing my attention to the stars in his eyes. "No more lies, no more secrets. I promise," he says, seriously.

"You break that promise, you'll have to find a spot on your body for the tattoo I'll demand," I softly warn while calling out for him with my eyes.

Grinning from ear to ear, he agrees. Gradually, a seductive expression takes hold of his features. "I have a question," he mouths, his voice barely loud enough to cover the wind. As he exhales, the hot air delicately comes into contact with my skin. I gulp loudly, as if trying to swallow the desire.

Sighing, I'm getting more and more worked up by the mere sight of him above me. *Just a little twitch, and the necklace drops on my face,* I think to myself. I hum to tell him to continue. Practically hypnotized by what lies beneath this shirt, I can't bring myself to form a word.

"Are you comfortable enough here?" he breathes out, almost grunting with effort. Frowning, I raise my line of sight and I'm met with a man doing his best to control himself from taking me savagely. "Is the ground too rough?" he questions.

Breathing through my open mouth, I mutter a *'no'* that would be perceptible only if he was looking at it. A part of me is lying—the rocks under my back are digging through my clothes—but I couldn't care less when the sound of his fly opening is enough for me to forget even my name.

Lowering his head, he kisses my lips before gluing his cheek to mine. "I want your mouth on me, Jade. Are you okay with it?" he speaks in a raspy voice.

"Yes," I moan. "But promise you'll bite me again."

"Everything you want, my girl."

Leaving a last brush of his lips on mine, Aidan straightens up to get back on his knees, letting my wrist go. I lower my arms and rest them on his thighs, making them course the length of it. Fascinated by him looming over, I can't detach my gaze from his body sitting on mine. His left hand plunges inside his pants to cup the under of his crotch while the other works on his erection, which contour I can clearly see through his underwear. While I squirm in place as he strokes himself, I take turn peering at his movements and his expression—his irises don't let me go for a second.

Feeling courageous, I reach for the hem of my shirt and slowly drag it over my body to expose my bra. Aidan's jerking becomes quicker when he ultimately loses the battle against himself and lowers his boxer to let his cock spring free from the pressure. My mouth is watering with the need to have him inside of me. So, I grab his jeans by the crease of his knees and lightly pull it toward me.

He drags his legs over the ground, drawing my arms with him until his bottom is over my chest area. His cock aligns with my face, and my mouth opens instinctively. I blow on it softly when he grabs the base and lowers it to my lips. "You're beautiful, Jade," he breathes out.

I lower my gaze to his crotch, watching the veins pulsate so close to me. I raise my chin and kiss the skin under, then take my tongue out and flick his crown twice—tasting the saltiness already accumulating on his tip. Aidan remains immobile, letting me decide what I want to do with him, though I'd like to be fully under his control.

"Force me. Do whatever you want," I plead.

He grunts in response, then smirks, clearly craving me. The torment is over, he clenches the hair on top of my head to guide my mouth to his penis. I open wide, but I can't properly prepare my jaw when, in one motion, he penetrates me. The saliva in my throat makes me gurgle, but being at his mercy makes my eyes roll into their sockets.

He breathes heavily but doesn't go too hard yet, only giving me a little past his tip and retracting, letting me have a taste, all the while driving me crazy with his stare seemingly diving into my soul.

The warmth of his delicate skin on my tongue almost makes me go feral, and I'd do anything to have him in my mouth forever. I can feel his veins on my lips, the heartbeat gently warning me of his excitement if the obvious erection wasn't enough.

Determined to give myself completely to him, I raise my arms above my head and cross my wrists, as he did earlier. Instantly, his hand, that was holding his base, comes over my head to keep me in place. His fingers entwine with mine, monopolizing enough of my senses to not go past that point of consciousness and become a wreaking mess too quickly.

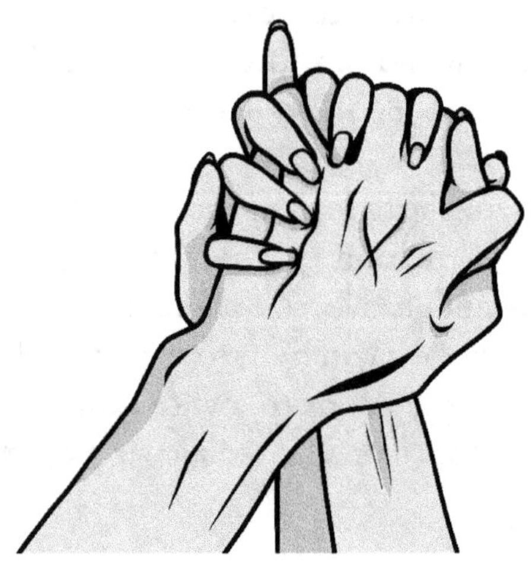

His gasps turn into growls when his body, now bent over my head, gives him a better angle to thrust his cock deeper. Involuntarily, I gag when he teases the back of my mouth. My breathing is impossible to control, I'm left heaving painfully as the tears progressively drown my eyes.

Afraid he might have hurt me, Aidan raises his haunches to let me catch my breath. "Breathe through your nose, not your mouth, baby," he instructs. He's patient with me and waits until I give him a clear sign that I'm ready again, to gradually lower himself inside of my mouth. This time, I take a full inhale through my nose and follow his motion with my hair to raise my chin to open up my throat for him.

Multiple times, his cock teases my tongue, my palate, before it goes all the way back to bury himself completely. Even though I'm not the one receiving pleasure, I can feel it in my core. I choke occasionally, but the thrusting and hair pulling have me aroused like I've never been before. I make my throat vibrate with a moan, which elicits one back from him. Loving the sensations, Aidan goes faster, planting his knees by my shoulders. He uses my head to pleasure himself, and I can't help but love watching him this way. Raising his hips, he gives me a couple of seconds to breathe, and thrusts back down. He strains his body and makes sure I'm thoroughly used.

My mouth is wide, my jaw hurts slightly, but nothing matters. I taste him and swallow as much as humanly possible. When he dives, and his hairs tingle my nose, not even then I could tell him to stop. He curses but never once leaves my eyes. Where I can see the story unfolding as the time passes—the desire, the primal need, morphing into desperation. His jaw is clenched, his hair disheveled, and a faint shine of sweat covers his exposed skin.

He thrusts with abandon, praises how good I feel. My legs squeeze together in answer. The cold air traveling under my skirt to freeze the already damp material of my panties.

The dirt under that was hurting me before is only an added touch of stimuli for my body. Using my mouth like he does, powerfully yet gently at the same time, makes me struggle under his weight to follow his action. I push on my legs to hopefully take him before he even lowers himself again.

The sounds he makes create the most beautiful music to my ears. Knowing I'm responsible for his pleasure gives me enough confidence to let go and explore my own with him. As some places we've slept together suggest, what truly matters to him—and to me—is how it feels in the moment. The bridge was perfect because it aligned with our need to drag the night as much as we could. Here in the forest, it's magical because when we're alone, it doesn't feel like it's just sex anymore.

He and I are more than friends, we're becoming a pair. A *whole*.

Gently, he unclenches his fist from my hair and lays my head on the ground. "Jade," he whimpers, preventing himself from doing anything and remaining impossibly still. "If I continue, I'll finish in your mouth." Already sore, I can't form any words, so I nod. Part aware, part agreeing. A hum follows when he unties his fingers from mine so I can lower my arms and wake my sleeping muscles.

Understanding what I'm trying to convey, he chuckles softly. "But I don't want to come in your mouth, baby," he coos. "Are you okay?" he asks.

"Yes," I utter, my voice cracking, making me smile, amused. Licking my lips while staring at his cock, I'm ready for more. Though, Aidan straightens back up and lifts his leg to sit by my side. Confused, I'm about to question him when he takes his shirt off. Swallowing back the comment, I'm left to stare at how perfect he looks in the night. Like a painting, I've never seen anyone so gorgeous before. It's not about the nudity in itself, but the simple beauty of his body. More than being attractive, Aidan is funny, playful, and has this gift of making me instantly calm when he's around.

"Come here," he motions for me to stand on my knees. When I do, he takes my shirt off, and I wait patiently while he positions each clothes on either side of his hips, the perfect placement for me to kneel on. Once again, I look around for any presence, but it appears we'll remain alone for as long as we wish for. Only *us*.

Before I straddle him, I lift my skirt to show him my stockings, all proud of myself for choosing a pair that's attached via strings and not full-on tights. He smirks and reaches for my crotch to trace the contour of my lips.

"I want it so bad. Let me have it," I mumble.

He finally pulls my panties aside and reaches for his pocket to retrieve the condom he must have taken when we got out of our cars. I watch with interest when he glides the rubber along his length, my arousal never going down. If anything, it's more heightened now than it was before.

"I know, baby. Come now." His palms come under my clothes to hold on to my hips. Like this, he guides me to him. I lift on my knees and slowly take him fully inside my cunt, embracing the sensation I've come to adore over the days by his side.

With both hands on his shoulders, I roll my pelvis on him to add more friction. "Oh, yes. Finally—" Together, we work to please the other while being selfish with our needs.

"There's something about you when we're in the middle of nowhere," he marvels, his breathing and groaning softly in unison with my own noises. He watches hypnotized as the strength of my thighs raises my body on my knees and drops on him repeatedly. Taking him every time a little deeper than before. I kiss his lips and smile at him when his hands leave my skirt to wrap on my back, bringing me closer to his skin. We share the warmth, the air, the feeling.

Swallowing is still difficult, as my throat is still dry. "It's the night. It's the stars, Aidan," I whisper. The sun goes down, and everything is ten times more intense, vivid. The sounds are sharper, the intimacy better.

"I think it's you," he confesses, his lips brushing against the bruise he left on my neck.

My heart skips a beat as his words resonate with my own unspoken desires. But I push the thought to the back of my mind, knowing that acknowledging what we have is greater than mere attraction is intimidating.

Instead, I pull his head closer and kiss him fervently, hoping to distract him.

As we move together, I find pleasure in the rhythm of our bodies. His hold on my back remains strong, his grip on my nape asserts his possessiveness. I moan into his mouth when he bites me. The expert strokes of his cock drive me closer to the edge, my awareness fading as I approach orgasm. "Aidan, it feels so good," I cry out, nearly screaming. Chanting his name in my head, while my dripping hole squeezes his shaft, stroking him similar to what my mouth and tongue did earlier.

Our passion escalates, our movements betraying out impatience. No longer concerned with pacing ourselves, we give in to the raw intensity of our craving. A primal need fueled by Aidan's words of encouragement, urging me to let go completely. "You're amazing. It's perfect. Go on, baby, come on," he praises.

"Just like that," I cry out as my climax washes over me, Aidan holding me close as I ride out the waves. I'm uncoordinated and wild, but it doesn't prevent him from crashing my hips to his and forcing me to remain still when he comes.

As I open my eyes to the stars above, a grin spreads across my face, quickly replaced by a hiss of pain when I feel the toll our hunger has taken on my body.

"You're alright," Aidan whispers, his eyes still closed in exhaustion. I press a kiss to his forehead, smiling at his sleepy expression.

Chuckling, I brush my lips over his eyelids where the words *'dead'* and *'end'* are. A simple caress is enough to bring a smile to his face. "Are *you*?" I laugh, still breathless.

He nods, joining in my amusement. "Maybe next time we should do it in a bed? I can't feel my ass," he complains, prompting a carefree laughter from us both, the sound echoing through the quiet night and awakening some birds from their nests nearby.

the hunt

CHAPTER 10

On the Streets of Greensburg.

War is not welcome in Greensburg. Being in the city limits could put his life in danger, Aidan explained. War, born in one of the districts, has a heavy past. He has done terrible things that led him to flee to Ursley. The rumors even suggested he was involved with the Madd Ryder. Since then, War has been gathering intel on the mafia families battling for control in the Business City, but his efforts became increasingly dangerous as he took a closer interest in their activities.

Tonight, however, I had a more pressing concern: the first mission assigned by War's inner circle. Despite the threats, I agreed to take part in the competition, partly because I was promised money at the end.

I know I'm risking my life, but Aidan assured me our tasks would usually keep us out of the spotlight, working in the shadows to follow War's orders.

As Aidan told me and the other three candidates, we'll have to outdo ourselves if we want to be the only winner in the end. It's a challenge that both terrifies and excites me, the adrenaline already fueling my body. It's funny how much I've changed in just a few weeks. Not long ago, I couldn't even entertain the thought of getting involved in such a dangerous business. But now, I'm diving headfirst into the mafia conflict.

I've built my confidence over these past few weeks, thanks in no small part to Aidan's encouragement. His constant reminders that I'm enough and I'm capable have been like a breath of fresh air. The worries used to plague my mind—about rent, about being recognized by old friends—now, they're only distant thoughts.

I *am* enough.

I *am* capable.

This challenge—the *first* I consent to—shouldn't be too difficult to complete. We've been given a list with only two items on it, but the actual test lies in retrieving these objects within the time limit. Three hours, that's all we have to steal a VIP all-access card from the nightclub Verona and find a map of the tunnels in Greensburg. As strange as these items may seem, I can easily understand their value to someone like War, seeking more ways to penetrate the city and place his pawns strategically.

"I'll start with the map. It's going to be the easiest," I murmur in the enclosed space of the WRX, which I've had little time to familiarize myself with during the trip from Ursley's garage to Greensburg. "Besides, what's the point of having you with me if you can't do anything?" I ask Aidan in the passenger seat, crossing his arms and feeling as bored as ever.

"I'll be your side-kick," he jokes, to which I grimace.

"Do the others have a babysitter too?" I tease, knowing he isn't here to keep an eye on me but because he wanted to spend time with me. Our peculiar jobs demand we be available at any moment, mostly outside normal working hours, leaving us with little time alone. Our version of a date involves street racing, secret competitions, and late-night car repairs, rather than a dinner at a nice restaurant and a movie. But I'm happy just being with him. We may not follow the conventional relationship rules, but it works for us, and that's what matters most.

He hums, thinking. "Not exactly."

I figure as much. "Can I hope for some nudging if I'm stuck?" I tempt, hopeful he'll have my back if I end up in jail for the night.

"No, no, no," he declares, motioning his index finger in the air with exaggeration. "You're on your own, little driver. I'm just a spectator," he announces proudly.

"Talk about a friend," I mumble to myself.

Suddenly, he gasps loudly, which startles me, thinking I've made a mistake and crossed a red light. "*We're friends?*" he exclaims, faking elation in an obnoxiously theatrical way.

I pinch my lips to contain the smile that wants out. I will not give him the satisfaction of playing into his childish games.

"Jade." He snaps his fingers playfully, attempting to capture my attention, but my eyes remain fixed on the road. "Baby, you want to be my friend?" he coos, a stupid grin contorting his face gorgeously. His sculpted cheeks, perfect almond-shaped eyes, and plump lips brighten and charmingly enhance his simple expression.

"Not anymore," I complain, now biting my lip to keep my mouth closed.

"*This*!" He points at my face. "I love that. When you try not to smile and your nose scrunches like that, yeah, that's so cute. You're adorable, you know that?" At his almost threatening tone, daring me to contest what he said, I burst out laughing. It's amazing how he can turn the most casual ambiance into a memory I'll cherish forever. Being with him feels like being with someone you've known all your life. It makes my heart flutter.

"I'm supposed to be focusing, you can't do that," I whine, still chortling.

This part of Greensburg is practically deserted at this hour. Months ago, I would spend the first half of my night near the business district, where people coming out of work would head directly to the lively area. They'd go to the nightclubs, fancy restaurants, and priceless hotels. Routine rules over every life, shifting which zone should have its moment for the next period. This never misses, and I know it for sure because I've witnessed it for as long as I can remember. Knowing my way around and all these little details allow me to know *when* and *where* I should act.

"I can. Like I said, I won't solve the dilemmas for you, but I'll do everything I can to make sure you're successful at it," he says, seriously. "And that includes making sure you don't feel nervous or lose your confidence. If making you laugh is all it takes to sharpen your attention, then *I will make you laugh,*" he vows.

The smile effectively wiped away from my lips, I park in reverse in the dark alley, knowing it won't attract any curious night-strollers. Killing the engine and taking off my seatbelt, I shift my body to face Aidan, who hasn't moved. "Thank you," I whisper. It strikes me how attentive he's been. I thought I was doing a good job concealing my emotions, especially when I felt anxious, but apparently not to him. He saw and understood how crippled I could feel at times, so he adapted his attitude to make sure I felt comfortable again.

The race at the Apocalys District, I remind myself. I felt incredibly worried and unsure if I'd even make it to the starting line. I didn't even realize back then Aidan tried to distract me as best as he could—by focusing on him and awakening my competitiveness rather than what made me scared.

Moving his body to face me, he raises his hand and holds my jaw, caressing my skin with his thumb as he slowly draws me to his lips. "It's what friends do, right?" he utters softly.

At a loss for words, I simply nod and kiss him again.

Parked here, we're supposed to wait until my competitors have also reached my city. I know most have taken the highway to reach the center, as coming into Greensburg via the North is an uncommon and unknown route. It's not a practical path, but it's damn fast. This advantage gives me extra few minutes on the other drivers, as they have to find their way around the labyrinth of districts to find the nightclubs, and they have to figure out where the old map might be.

A notification chimes from Aidan's phone in his hand. Both our heads turn to it; I can read War's name on it. "The timer starts now," Aidan announces.

"How does he know we haven't started already?" I ask, baffled and slightly scared of the reach the boss might have over all of us. It even prompts me to look at the buildings around. Could an apartment be used by one of his spies?

"There're GPS trackers in your car. There's also a custom-made device wired to the electrical system of the Subaru linked to your door ajar sensor on your side. Like that, War has real-time information about your whereabouts. Including when the doors open and close," he explains in a single breath.

I freeze, my hand gripping the handle. "Are you serious? *What is that?*" I blurt out, my voice betraying my shock. "We live in the *real* world—those types of tech shouldn't exist."

Aidan smirks, the corner of his lips curling amusedly. "When you know the right people, they do."

Eyes widening, I take more time than I should to observe the door opening. Nothing points to a hidden black market device inside. As quickly as the thought arises, I push it aside. I don't have time to ponder the *how*—I need to find that map.

"So, what's your plan?" Aidan asks by my side, surveying the area and the building right across the road.

I send a playful smile his way. "Well, the reason I wanted to start with the map was because I know for a fact that it's in the public library." I point at the façade behind him. "More precisely, in the archive area in the basement," I reveal, crossing the street to reach the entrance stairs.

"*Okay,*" he stretches the syllables. "How are you going to trespass?"

Proud of myself, I fish out the key to the maintenance door at the back and show it to him. "Enter through the door?" I say, obviously. Some cars pass by, prompting me to take Aidan's hand and quickly drag him to the back. After letting him go, I check around for any cameras, but it seems the past events haven't made them more alert.

"You're going to make me ask you, aren't you?" he grunts behind me.

Smiling to myself, I insert the key, and unsurprisingly, the door opens. "I used to work here when I was in high school. Since I preferred the evening shifts, I was always the one closing the library. At night, I'd invite some friends over. Long story short, a party happened, and I got fired," I whisper as I walk up the staircase to the main hall, Aidan following closely behind.

"You never told me you were the troublemaking type," Aidan's sweet voice reaches my ear. My steps slow involuntarily as I feel his body heat on my back. "What else are you not telling me, Jade?" he whispers into my ear, brushing my hair back, his warm breath tingling the skin of my neck.

I'm aware he wants to be charming and playful. He doesn't have ill intent with his words, yet it's the opposite happening in my brain. In response, my muscles tense.

I am a murderer.

The face of the girl who lost her life because of me appears in my head. But I can't erase the past or go back to change what I did. "I used to drink too much and party when I should've studied," I say, distancing myself from him and walking around the counter to reach the staff door leading to the basement where the archives should be. "How were you in high school?" I ask to shift the attention away from me.

Both of us descend another staircase, and I lead the way to the small office below. If I remember correctly, the keys to open the pad and enter the code should be in the first drawer. So, I go behind the desk and find them exactly where they were years ago. The best things about establishments directed by an older generation are habits never change, rules remain, and codes are always '1,2,3,4.'

"Oh, I was totally different. You would've hated me. Small kid, shy, and never talked," he confesses in a tone suggesting he regrets those times when things were easier.

I position myself in front of the open pad, but instead of entering the combination, I turn around to face him. "I might have been different from you, but I never preyed on someone. Never made fun of someone. If you had come to this library to return a book and started a conversation with me, I would've listened."

Aidan moves closer, crosses his arms over his chest, and bends over to kiss my cheek. Instead of pulling away, he whispers as softly as he can. "I appreciate your honesty, baby, but trust me when I say you would've hated me." Rising to his full height again, I see in his eyes he thinks it's truth, despite the kind smile and relaxed attitude. "I spent most of my teenage years in juvie."

It explains a lot, yet raises more questions. "What happened?" I ask, empathizing with his story.

"I was shy and small, but the big guys knew I was damn good at stealing catalytic converters," he shrugs.

Cats—as they're also called—are a seemingly insignificant part of a car, yet they hold a lot of value in the aftermarket. His friends and him must have been influenced and forced to steal for those guys. "I'm sorry," I say, lifting my arm to touch his elbow. After squeezing once and releasing the tense air from our lungs, we both nod in understanding. We'll have all the time in the world to talk after the competition. For now, I must hurry.

"The map should be in there. I'll take a picture of it and send it directly to War," I announce, rushing into the archive room without waiting for Aidan.

time out

CHAPTER 11
Verona Club in Greensburg.

"What if I just buy one?" I wonder out loud. Sure, a VIP access card must cost a fortune, but at least it will save me a lot of trouble and I'll end up finishing first.

"Can't give you the solution, but *hey*," Aidan calls out to get my attention. When I do, he points a finger at his chin and shakes his head from left to right.

This week is Greensburg's centennial celebration. As a result, all roads leading to any parts of the nightlife district are closed for cars. I had to park the WRX too far from our destination and walk all the way to the Verona club. "No one gave us any rules, did they?" My fingers brush the short dress I changed into in the car, checking my heels to make sure they're tightly fastened on my ankles in case of an emergency escape where I'll have to run. On my side, Aidan didn't bother to wear the dress shirt I brought for him.

"We didn't, but we're not only testing your driving skills. Remember that." Of course, all of them are involved in some sort of criminal activities, and if I join them and refuse to do anything remotely illegal, I won't last long. With this plan fully out of the picture, I'll have to change my strategy.

I stop a couple of steps away from the club. The line is long, the two bouncers look threatening, and I have no idea how I'll get in without waiting in the queue. I wonder how the others managed, or if some are still there. So far, I've only seen Rafael, Luca, and Marcus at the meeting with War's inner circle. I wasn't sure if talking with them and getting to know them was a good idea, so I quickly fled the place when it was done. Maybe if I hadn't been so awkward, I would've managed to form an alliance with one of them and find a solution.

"I don't know what to do," I whisper to myself, looking around at the many faces, feeling the nervousness flowing through my veins. "I don't know," I repeat again, the sentiment written all over my features.

I take out my phone and scroll absentmindedly, opening and closing apps to get my mind out of the situation and hopefully awaken a brilliant idea. Suddenly, Aidan's hand grabs onto my nape and lifts my head to his. Completely calm and master of himself, he crashes his lips to mine. As if dancing to the same melody once again, my body reacts instantly, holding onto his shirt to keep him close. His other hand comes to my face and covers the side of it, lacing his fingers into my flowing hair, dancing with the wind.

His tongue finds mine, circling it while teasing with his teeth the delicate skin of my lips. Tasting him feels like eating sweets—it gives this familiar feeling, almost like being nostalgic. Aidan is my friend, the man who easily makes me laugh, he's also the one who makes the butterflies flutter in my stomach.

I have to breathe again, but he doesn't give me a chance. Instead, he lowers his hands from my head to clutch my waist, firmly maintaining me glued to him. I have no choice but to savor what he's giving me. This soft moment in the middle of the nightlife chaos all around us.

Gently, he moves back and breaks our connection. He doesn't utter a word after that.

"Thank you," I mouth, knowing it was yet another distraction to bring me back from inside my head. He winks.

Think, think.

I have never been to this club before. This one, compared to the Balkans, is a lot more exclusive. It only allows people with perfect appearances. Trying to go in the normal way will not get me far. That, I already knew.

I have two solutions: going in accompanied or sneaking in.

Since being discreet isn't really my specialty, I'll have to find someone or preferably a group to insert myself into. Yet, even then, not being noticed would be impossible. I grew up here, I've known this area my whole life. If there is someone deserving of completing this mission it's *me*.

From the corner of my eyes, I see a group of five men coming out of Verona's building corner, from the adjacent street. All are distracted, laughing, smoking, talking. Which gives me an idea. Smiling, I turn to Aidan, apparently already aware of what's inside my head by the smirk he wears.

"Technically, you're only asking for a lighter. I'll do everything," I convince him.

He exhales loudly, taking a cigarette out of his pocket. "No, Jade, I'm helping. Which I'm not supposed to be doing, yet here I am. But you learn fast, people like War play around with the rules on the daily," he snorts to himself.

Happy with how easy this whole convincing was, I raise on my toes and plant a kiss on his lips before I hurry to cross the road and position myself right behind the men. They are talking animatedly about the stock market, a conversation I'm quick to mute in order to focus on their coats. Long, black, and oversized, perfect for sliding my hand in and retrieve what I'm looking for. My only hope is they all have their cards in their pockets and not inside their suits.

Ready and in place, they walk toward to the back entrance, where most VIPs are expected considering their high status. In time, as if summoned, Aidan appears right in front of them. Barely visible, glued to the wall by their sides, I keep my body covered in shadows and only extend my hand when Aidan breaks their discussion and brings all eyes on him.

"Good evening. Sorry to bother you. May I ask for a lighter, please?" Aidan articulates while exaggerating his friendly smile.

I don't waste any time—my hand quickly plunges inside the first man's coat and looks for anything feeling like a card on the tip of my fingers. Unfortunately, I don't find any. My heart somehow beats faster than during a race. I retrieve my hand and immediately look inside another one.

"Of course," the man right in front of him says, getting his own lighter out. "There you go." Aidan lights his cigarette, but the wind blows the flame away before he has time to ignite the stick. This might be his way of dragging the distraction.

This time, in the third coat, I finally feel what I'm looking for. Not pondering anymore, I get the card out, glimpse at it, and crash my back into the wall again.

Suddenly, Aidan is now successful at lighting his cigarette. "Thank you. Have a great night."

"You too," the man replies.

I watch as my friend crosses the road back again and waits for me there, puffing on his umpteenth cigarette of the night. I wait a few more seconds until the group joins the club before slipping away unnoticed. With the mission over, Aidan and I will head to my place for the night. I'm already longing for the hot shower waiting for me.

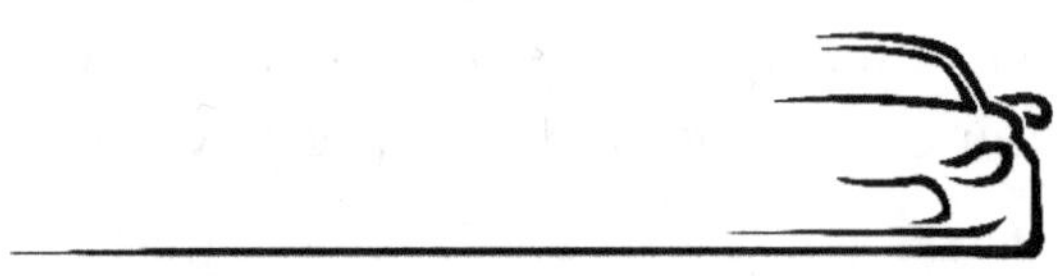

Hands submerged into the water as I wash the dishes, my breath catches when I hear the soft padding of Aidan's feet approaching. Distracted, I grab a plate and mindlessly scrub its already clean surface. My eyes flutter closed as his strong arms wrap around my waist, his hands flattening over my stomach. "You did a great job tonight," Aidan murmurs, his nose nuzzling the delicate skin behind my ear. His warm exhale has my loose hair dance.

"Let's not talk about it. I need a time out," I implore. The stress accumulating from these past few days reaching a point where it has become impossible to relax without intrusive thoughts.

My hand stops polishing the ceramic when the smoothness of his lips starts trailing kisses along my neck. I tilt my head to the side, giving him more access. Aidan cups my braless breasts to knead them gently, causing the tension to rise in the non-existent space between us. He pauses to press his pelvis against mine, pushing me against the kitchenette of my apartment. Water stains my oversized shirt, and I drop the plate to grip the edge of the sink. Her tender breaths and the gentle sway of his hips relax me like a full night's sleep.

I need this escape, and Aidan seems to understand completely. "No talking, got it. I know just what you crave," he whispers huskily, nibbling on my earlobe. I join his dance, whimpering as electricity shocks us every time we touch. His bulge pokes at my bottom through our skimpy clothing, swelling with blood as I arch my back to press against it. My body startles upon hearing, *feeling,* the animalistic groan that comes out of his mouth.

"Stay like this," he commands roughly, his legs shifting to squeeze my mound painfully against the counter's edge. I comply, clenching my jaw to resist looking back. His fingers capture the hem of my shirt, peeling the wet material from my body. The cool ambient air immediately tightens my nipples, teasing their sensitivity. His strokes ignite a fire within me, banishing all thoughts of what has happened since we met. The race, the competition—none of it matters. Not when his hands trace the curve of my chest, sliding down to tug at the elastic of my underwear. The lingerie falls on the tiles, my breath hitches as I stand naked before him.

Aware his gaze devours me, I resist looking back, eager to see where he will take us. His bare torso brushes gently against my back, his hands resuming their exploration. Finally, he locks an arm over my ribcage while the other caresses me as it moves down. Then his palm reaches between my legs that I spread unconsciously. A gasp followed by a moan escape my mouth at the first flick of his middle finger on my clit. He fondles my slit with expert movements while his covered cock nestles perfectly between my cheeks.

"Aidan—" I cry out, the squelching sounds of my slick dripping over his wrist add to the intensity of his fingering. He shushes me, asking me to enjoy him and focus on his touch.

I lose his warmth for a second as he lowers his boxers. I bite my lip, trying to be patient when my sanity wavers with the desperation of having him inside me. But the reminder of our lack of protection flashes through my mind. At every occasion I have been reliant on him and didn't bother to buy anything. "Wait, we can't," I twist around suddenly, just as he was about to slap my behind with his cock. My eyes widen at the redness of his erection and him using his saliva to lube himself with.

His smirk doesn't falter, his intense gaze rake over my body as he resumes his ministrations, shamelessly pumping himself. His stare runs from my head, lingering on my mouth, down to the apex of my thighs—glistening under the soft moonlight casting a bluish hue over the small apartment. The dim lamp barely illuminates the space, it's as if everything here was meant to create a dreamlike ambience.

"There are other ways, baby. Don't worry about it," he assures me, his cockiness matching both his character and actions. I gulp at the implication, the night at his place when I could have died perched on his window frame comes to mind.

His breathing quickens and I understand what he means. Extending my arm toward him, I rest two fingers on his lower lip. "Suck." His stare darkens with passion and need as he opens his mouth, welcoming my digits on his tongue. He sucks on them as his other hand moves to massage his balls. His vision seems unfocused when he spits on my hand as I retrieve it. I swallow, my throat dry, as I slowly lower my wet fingers to my cunt, trembling with need as I make contact with my velvety lips. The atmosphere becomes heated, our erotic sounds setting the pace. My mouth is agape as I watch Aidan pleasuring himself with a familiarity I want to learn. His chest rises and falls rapidly observing my hand making circles over my sensitive spot, gradually lowering it and empaling myself until my knuckles disappear.

"Spread your legs," he directs breathlessly, breaking the silence. With little room in my studio, I drop to the floor, resting my back against the counter and opening my knees as far as I can. Aidan curses when my wetness drools out, offering myself for his eyes only.

I gesture with my chin for him to join, but his amusement grows. He watches me with desperate hunger as I tease and fuck myself. "Aidan, please. Aidan, baby—" His name becomes a prayer that I chant when my body coaxes me toward release. Aidan steps closer, his cock proudly standing as he never stops stroking himself. My mouth parts, expecting to taste him, expecting the saltiness I've craved since last time. I want to feel his throbbing member, but he grunts in warning, denying me.

I plead with my eyes, the thrusting inside my soaking pussy accelerates. My eyebrows knit in desperation as he hovers over me, resting a hand on the sink's edge and lowering his head. His cock, right in front of my face, tempts me to stick my tongue out. Just a tilt of my neck and I'll have his tip on my lips. Yet he bends slightly over, keeping his hips too far for my face but close enough for me to smell him. "You like that a lot, don't you, sweetheart?" he taunts.

I spread my legs over his shins, opening myself further in response, letting the charged air tease my sensitivity. Fog clouds my mind, my heart races, and I drop my head back, watching my man above me. His smile is too sweet for what we are doing.

"Baby. My Jade," he mouths silently. The veins on his forehead betray his strain, his teeth gritting. The smallest movement of his hips has his crown touch under my jaw, tipping my sanity over the edge. My body trembles as the climax washes over me, my hand rubbing my clit thoroughly to drag the euphoria a little more. My eyes roll back, ears buzzing with my release, until I feel hot spurts of cum on my throat, dripping over my chest, running along my stomach.

When I open my eyes, Aidan is resting his forehead on the top of my head. I raise my arms, circling what I can of his torso, obliging him to crouch between my legs. "You're incredible," I praise, grinning with utter satisfaction.

He kneels, letting out a breathy chuckle and quickly pecking my nose. "How are you feeling?" he asks, his breath still uneven. His expression brightens when I reach for his hair, brushing it back and scratching his scalp affectionately.

"I'm feeling very, *very* good," I announce, my cheek muscles aching to accommodate the bright smile.

We sit there for a long moment, the world outside my small studio apartment forgotten. Contempt and overall happiness having my body relaxed to the point of yawning. For the first time I'm ready to go to bed and sleep a full night.

"You're sleepy," he points out, surprised like me. Frowning, I get ready to contest. However, another yawn crushes my attempt. "Let's clean up, and we'll get you to bed," he says, but the playful glimmer in his eyes and the way he gulps while surveying my torso painted with his release tells me he has other plans once we are under the covers.

most wanted

CHAPTER 12
In Ursley.

One of my legs jumps in place, my limbs grow tense, and I can't help but checking my phone every few seconds, unlocking it and putting it back on the table in front of me. The cup of coffee I ordered earlier does nothing to calm the disastrous scenarios unfolding in great detail in my head. They were clear on that matter—if a cop finds you, you're on your own. That goes without saying War will not move a muscle to come get us out, and we'll be eliminated from the competition. On top of that, we're expected not to rat everyone out.

In my short driving career, risks have always been a part of what I do. Though the races were short enough and organized in a way that left little to no room for the police to interfere. Now, I have a feeling both War and the circle—including Aidan—have prepared something to test us. Not in the way they've been doing so far, but something drastic to quickly get rid of the weak candidates.

The last mission was a success for *all* of us. I managed to be the first to achieve it, but the others weren't far behind. Besides, most didn't bother with the rules and simply stole the VIP cards without elaborate plans. They were sneaky and quick—not resourceful, like I was. As a result, the circle had to find a way to put us all on equal footing to really *see* which ones they need to remove.

My favorite mechanic called me some days ago, telling me we couldn't see each other before the end of this mission. Normally, I wouldn't be so fazed by it, but recently Aidan's presence grew on me. I couldn't see it before, but not having him around really takes away the sense of calm and happiness to which I've become familiar with.

I know it's dangerous to be this dependent on someone, yet it still makes me sad, sadder than I've been after I lost all my friends. This, I was prepared for but not with Aidan. Not talking to him or seeing his face has demolished every progress I've made on myself. How will I ever win my place in War's inner circle if I don't believe I'm talented enough?

The buzzing of my phone against the glass table tears me away from my head. I'll have to go through with it because they left me no other choice. I will not return to what I was doing before because the taste of adrenaline is too much to go without. Being a private chauffeur isn't satisfying enough. I *want* to be a part of something greater, to work and be recognized as someone valuable.

Your target is at the Florence Hotel. Black leather coat, round glasses, blond hair. I'll wait for you at the warehouse, little driver. Make me proud, Aidan messages me.

Without wasting time, I leave the campus coffee shop—where they told me I should wait—and run to the parking lot where one of my dream cars waits for me. An all-white 370Z, one of the three other identical ones my competitors have. To test the drivers' skills, there's nothing like putting them all in equal machinery.

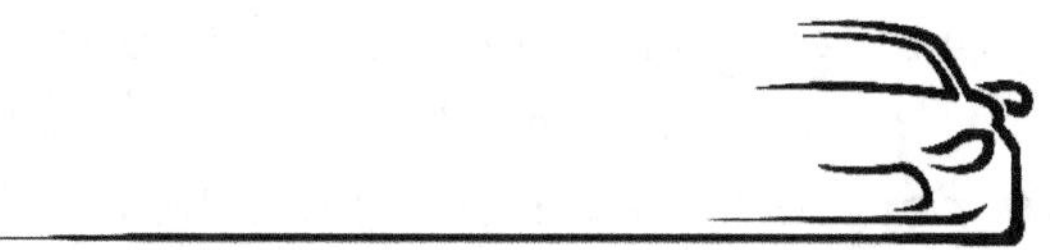

In the hotel's lobby, I frantically look around for the guy matching the description. Everything about this mission feels like a simulation, I know that much. It teaches me about what is expected of a driver working for War—getting his spies from point A to point B as quickly as possible.

A man sits on a velvet chair by the artificial pond, reading the newspaper. Quickly, I check the message, and it seems he's the one I'm looking for. Scanning the room, I decide it's best to confirm rather than waste time.

With long strides, I approach him and wave my hand. When he looks up, I smile kindly. "It's not too cold outside. How about a stroll in the park instead of reading?"

The man nods, acknowledging the code given by the circle yesterday. "You're right, it would be a waste. Will you join me?" he replies, reciting word-for-word what was written on the script.

Prompting him to follow me, I turn around and leave the lobby. Other than him, it seems no one else is aware of what's happening. Thankfully, I can now rule out the possibility of my boss having people watching over me and noting my every move. This kind of pressure I can't take. I know he can access my location at any time with the trackers he probably has in all of our 370Z, but seeing shadows would be too much effort to filter out, to focus on the job.

"I'm parked right in front," I tell the man, pointing at the car. Without waiting for him, I hurry to walk around and settle into the driver's seat while he gets in beside me. He buckles up, and after that he doesn't utter a word, respecting my need to concentrate on the ride.

Just to be sure I quickly glance at my mirrors before putting the car in first gear and leaving the hotel's minute-deposit.

For the first time, the mission happens during the day which means heavy traffic along the highway crossing over Ursley and the main road leading to the different college hubs. At night, there're some tricks a driver can adopt to become invisible—lights turned off inside the car, or license plates switched and hidden.

Most are not doable when the sun shines. This, coupled with the fact the Nissan's one of those cars easily spotted on the road, makes me a vulnerable target.

But I try not to get too caught up in envisioning all the ways this could go wrong. It's a simple mission after all: get the target, drive them to the warehouse as fast as possible, and *done*. I believe they're testing our ability to maneuver through traffic and find shortcuts to avoid it. Unlike when we were in Greensburg, I'm the one at a disadvantage here. I know Ursley well enough, but still far less than the other three drivers.

Turning to exit the city center to join the beltway, an alert immediately catches my attention on the GPS in front of me. On it, a member of the inner circle seems to have sent a message to all candidates. Glancing at the road then the GPS to read the message, my expression quickly morphs into one of horror when I understand the situation.

"Fuck," I curse. *"Fuck!"* I exclaim, hitting the steering wheel out of frustration. The man by my side chortles which has my head jerking in his direction to show how unfunny the whole situation is. "You'd better hold on tight," I sternly say, knowing I'll have a hard time thinking about his safety while having my eyes glued to the road ahead. It's what I need to do to get us out of this.

The test—the *real* one—has started.

Turns out, they never planned to make it easy for us. After all, only danger and stress can effectively separate the excellent driver from the plain wannabe. How better to test those skills than in a real-time simulation while putting us all in the same cars and alerting the police of a wild rodeo in preparation?

The preys and the predators. It's merely a game of cat and mouse, but if the mouse gets caught, the chase is guaranteed to end.

"I don't see any lights yet," the target informs me, looking around like I do.

I don't either but I know it's only a matter of time. Hence why they scattered us all in different parts of the city, to make the hunt greater and disorient the police by making them believe there might be a lot more 370Z on the road than only the four of us. "Will you tell me if you spot them?" I ask, my voice shaking with urgency.

"Sure. Not because I want to help, but if they get us, I'm falling too," he justifies.

Of course, that's what he'll say. "Fine by me."

I drive with precision, one hand ensuring I don't exceed the speed limit, but also because I feel my focus slipping. They expect me to outrun the pursuers while racing the others, all the while making sure I'm not followed so I can get my target to the warehouse.

It's too much—*way* too much. Yet it's too late to turn around and leave. I've gone too far to abandon everything like a coward. Working for War is my ultimate goal. His tests terrify me, but it's the price to pay for the life I've always wanted—one without worrying about money, one that would bring me a new family, a purpose. I've wandered too long in darkness, hated myself enough—I deserve to live my life too. It's hard to forgive my own faults but the first step would be acceptance.

I killed someone. I *am* responsible. Now, what can I do to make sure it never happens again? It's foolish to believe I won't make any mistakes. Truthfully, my partaking in this competition is dangerous enough to compromise other people's lives, and I'm a hypocrite. So, I will drive *better* than everyone else, remain sober for the rest of my life, and extend my focus not only to the race but also to the people around me. I will earn the spot in War's inner circle, and I will deserve it because I will deliver my target to the end location promptly and without causing accidents. This job is as important as ensuring no one dies.

"*Look,*" the blond man draws my attention.

Glancing into my rearview mirror, my eyes widen as I locate the source of his urgency—the lines of cars parting to leave a path in the middle of the beltway for the one flashing red and blue lights. The alarming speed at which it closes the gap has me gasping in panic. We've been identified. it's pointless trying to blend in with the rest of the traffic.

"Now, it's time for you to *hold on.*" I almost scream, unable to control my body and project my fears onto him.

My brain gauges the paths I could take at a blinding speed. In less time it takes to blink, I've already veered the car to the left to drive along the emergency lane. Stomping on the throttle, the traffic blurs in my peripheral vision. My heartbeat matches my gear changes.

The straight line offers the perfect escape route. Behind me, the lights grow further away. Though now they have no doubts I'm the one they're looking for. The split-second decision sharpens my focus on the only path I can take and the ones I have to avoid.

Soon, I'm confronted with an exit where cars are lined up, blocking my way across. Since going through them isn't an option, I take the way out. The rear-wheel-drive offers the perfect momentum to slide the 370Z through the curve, making the engine roar loudly. I almost rip my lips off biting them. Shifting again, I rejoin the city's complex grid layout.

The streets offer fewer opportunities to accelerate, but instead offer more to hide, outrun, and deceive, allowing me to see different paths toward the warehouse. Though the warehouse isn't the priority now, not when I'm being hunted down.

Racing through the green lights, I grip the steering wheel and never stray from my straight trajectory—the main street being an uninterrupted line is the only time I'll be able to gain some speed and put some distance between me and the cop behind.

Speaking of which, the red and blue lights have now *doubled*.

"Coming from the right," the target notifies me, and true enough, another car joins the chase.

By sliding the vehicle from left to right to gain momentum for the upcoming intersection and to confuse the police, the rear easily follows. I maneuver through the civilians to come face-to-face with a red light. The traffic doesn't lessen. The honks grow insistent. I brake faintly, but I can't fully stop as the threat behind are a reminder enough I won't be given a second chance or be slapped on the wrist. Being pulled over means finally meeting that jail bed with my name on it.

Choosing to dive right into the flowing traffic stops the beating of my heart. At this moment, the world seems to still, everything happens in slow motion—the drivers look at me in terror as they see my car missing theirs by just a hair's breadth. Harsh steering wheel jerks to avoid collision, and there're screams—so many screaming faces.

Abigail Holden screamed too.

My expression matches theirs, worthlessly attempting to show them I mean no harm.

The car continues to slide through the crossroad, avoiding them as best as I can, but guiding my wheels where I want them is harder than it looks. Bile rises in my throat. I have to hold on. This life, it's what I'm *made* for. Adrenaline is an old friend of mine—it never lets me down. So, I trust it and grit my teeth harder when I finally shift gears again and crush the throttle. On my left, a Corolla collides with a Raptor right in the nose.

"Jesus Christ," I sob when, in that split-second, I see the Toyota's front almost entirely under the Ford.

My panting turns into cries as tears gradually cover my vision. Yet, I must continue, focus, and get the target where it needs to be. Ursley streets are a mess, and if the other three are as desperate as I am to finish this race, I hope for the people's sake no one goes out.

Noticing the drivers I pass sending me death glares, I realize I must do something with my face. My windows have a filter, but it seems the circle thought it best to get a shade percentage within the legal limit. Meaning, it's still see-through, and my face is pretty much entirely visible.

"Look inside the glove—" A sob escapes my throat without much control, but I groan and temper my emotions down as much as I can. "The glove compartment. Something to hide our faces."

The blond guy hurries and looks for covers. A choked laugh takes over me when we both realize two surgical black masks were hidden. He quickly wears his, and I shift my body closer to his while maintaining my gaze on the road as he puts mine on.

"Thanks," I breathe out, not feeling like much air goes into my lungs.

He turns his head around us to look behind. His murmurs, while counting, reach my ear. "There're five now," he announces firmly. Is it the adrenaline in him that has his voice turning a pitch deeper, or the fear of getting caught because he agreed to be a pawn in this simulation with a complete stranger?

"I'll get us out of here," I assure him. It's clear to me now if I only focus on speed, I'll never lose those heavy wagons. I'll have to play them, *trap* them. Finally, the fog in my brain clears a little, giving me enough reason to form a plan.

I need to get deeper into the city, reach the part where the streets are narrower, the driveways open, and the city maze more complex.

"Sharp left," I warn him, two seconds before I yank the steering wheel to the left, sliding the car on the asphalt in a beautiful dance over the road. The screeching of the tires against the ground mixed with the vibration of the powerful V6 engine are enough to keep myself grounded and make one with the car despite having just met.

Not releasing the pressure on the throttle, I fly through the streets, turning left, right, going straight ahead, all this time without touching anyone in my path. I believe the other drivers are scared of me, dreading what I could do to them, but thankfully none try to make sudden movements. These would be fatal at high speed.

Still seeing the law enforcement in my mirrors, I have to make yet another split-second decision to avoid arrest. The target beside me doesn't show any signs of giving up—he remains calm as if he's already been through this before. Nothing on his features betrays his thoughts, which I'm again thankful for. Having him panic with me would be terrible for both of us.

It seems the police have changed strategies, not only pursuing us, but setting traps to stop me. An officer at the end of the road is getting ready to roll out his stop stick, hoping to puncture my tires and end the pursuit. But again, the good thing about this grid-kind of city plans means there's *always* another path.

"On your left, about a thousand feet away, there're the Art buildings. They wouldn't risk trying anything with the students around," he offers conversationally.

That's all it takes before I guide the car this way. At the last minute, I glimpse at the officer on foot and see him raising his hand in the air in defeat. This finally brings a small grin to my lips. A grin quickly wiped out when I realize I'll need to be extra careful because the students are now *everywhere*. There must be a thousand pedestrians now. My worst nightmare awakens, and I have to actively repress the gruesome images surging through my mind.

Out of nowhere, someone jumps onto the road to cross it. Immediately, I slam on the brakes but give my steering wheel a jerk to the right, sending the car sliding. We cut the man's path, and he jumps back, hitting his head on the pavement to avoid the accident.

The air empties out of my lungs, and I have a serious dizziness happening at the moment. "Coming here—was—a bad—*bad* idea," I choke out, panting and puffing through the mask, breathing my dioxide, which worsens the spinning-head effect.

"No, it's perfect," he joyously utters. "Fuck *yeah!*" he exclaims, checking all the windows.

Curious, I look back and see the police have been blocked by three buses coming right before the road-crossing section where the man is on the ground, surrounded by a mass of his peers.

I blow out the panted-up air but don't scream victory yet. I'll have to make sure I remain invisible. Only then will the way to the warehouse be safe. "I have a plan," I announce, not reducing my speed to take the next turn on my right. I know if I do what I have in mind the risk of being seen will go through the roof. But I don't have much choice—I hardly know any hideouts in Ursley apart from the ones I've already been to when I was studying here. So, I take every precaution necessary and only drive through the alleys and residential areas.

"Where are we going?" my target asks.

I slow down when I spot the house I used to rent here with my best friend. Before she threw me out and forgot about me. "There's a garage at the back. The gate's broken so we can go in without the code." This part of the city is where students usually rent cheaply. Most, I assume, are in class. I park the car in the driveway and engage the handbrake before going out—the mask still on. A quick look around only confirms what I've expected, and if it can remain that way for the next hour, it would be perfect for us.

I open the gate and quickly settle back in the driver's seat.

"Why are we waiting for? It only gives the cops more time to plan," the target angrily remarks, not trusting me.

A race sometimes means taking your time to evaluate your options. That's my strategy. "The city's attention is drawn to those 370Z. It's a manhunt at this point. I've done enough damage to worsen everything already." I sigh heavily as my conscious mind replays the accidents in a loop.

All parking spots are empty, and the house as well. I reverse into my old one and kill the engine. "I'm hoping they'll make mistakes. And when they do, I'll have a clear path to safely take you to the end location," I reveal my plan, feeling absolutely drained and hopeless.

"You're betting on professional drivers—competing to have a spot in the boss' circle—to make *mistakes*?" He puffs in mockery. "We're definitely getting arrested," he mutters to himself.

Yes, I'm a coward, and I have trouble sticking to one thought at a time. I'm only human. A moment I have a surge of confidence and believe I can achieve anything—have the spot I so desperately need— but at other times, I want the ground to swallow me whole. The pressure of existing is too much to bear. My goal is to be happy, forgive myself, have a future. I know I'm smart and capable, but how do I persuade my brain not to sabotage my efforts when things get too hard?

I could use a friend, the thought comes like a gentle caress, making its way through the fog of my emotions. Is it against the rules? It has to be, but Aidan trusts me. It's what I need to hear, despite knowing how dangerous the time I'm wasting might be.

"Stay in the car," I warn the blond guy. Not waiting for his answer, I open my door and slam it shut behind me. I pull out my phone from my back pocket and immediately search for Aidan's number.

The rhythmic beeping signals the call is coming through, which surprisingly plummets my mood. He may be angry at me, disgusted even. Is it really something I want to discover? *I still have time to hang up—*

"Jade, what are you *doing*?" Aidan's familiar voice echoes in my ears.

"I—" Cutting myself off, I pace in front of the car, looking for words. "Have you seen what I did?" I ask, uneasy.

"If I've *seen*—fuck—" he whispers-shouts. "The others are not that far, and I shouldn't be talking to you, but Jade. My *god,*" he breathes out into the microphone.

With the target still in his seat behind me, I sit on the hood and lower my head. "I'm sorry," I sob, hiding my face in my hand. He must think I'm a monster, not even stopping when causing an accident. Blinded to the point of putting multiple lives in danger.

"Sorry? You're *sorry*?" he repeats, astonished. "Baby, you had War on the edge of his seat. Even *he* was rooting for you, and you're mine! *My* fucking girl," he declares, still using this pressing tone as if he was in the car with me, feeling the adrenaline, too.

"What?" I can't believe it. *Rooting* for me? So, they liked what I did?

"You've taken all my expectations and smashed them against a wall. Everything you've done so far is perfect. *Perfect.* You're a fucking outstanding driver," he praises breathlessly, shaking my earlier self-doubt and transforming it back into one optimistic emotion, leaving me fidgety. "Baby, I don't know where you are right now; the helicopter stopped recording, and only War has all your locations, but you have to come to me now. I shouldn't tell you, but if you're the first here, it's secured. Marcus' out already. They had him on Frost Road where you left that mess behind. It doesn't look too good for Luca either," he informs me in a single breath, giving all the information I need to not lose hope and double my efforts for that last stretch. It turns out my cowardice strategy paid off—they *did* attract all the attention away from me.

"You're not mad at me?" I inquire, still having trouble believing everything. My muscles twitch with the need to release the tense atmosphere all around me, but I hold on for *him.* The soft murmur in my mind of my feelings for him circles until it's the only thing I can think of. "Aidan, I—I—"

"Mad at you? Of course not, you're amazing! Please don't tell me you're doubting yourself, not right now, little driver," he says threateningly somehow full of affection and care for me. That's how I interpret it, which is why I snort at his comment.

"I wouldn't dare," I whisper.

"Good, because I want you to get your head into the race. You shake those stupid thoughts out of your mind, you buckle up, and you show them how that Greensburg's girl managed to become one of the best street racers," he encourages, forever my number one supporter.

A smile tugs at my mouth, and I can't help but be grateful for our lives to have crossed in such a magnetic way. It's as if we couldn't help but be drawn and compelled to never let go. "I will. Thank you for everything, Aidan. I'll see you later," I murmur slowly, the smile ever so present.

"Remember, you come to *me*. Everything else is only dust."

When he hangs up, I slowly straighten up, the grin still stretching the muscles of my face. My heart races, finally ready to wrap this up. The police never catch me because Aidan is right: I'm one of the best.

And I'll prove it.

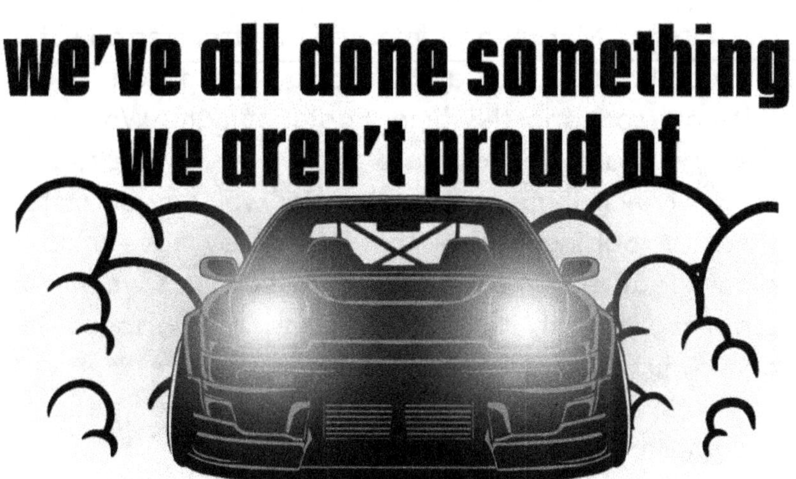

CHAPTER 13
In Ursley.

"How long before you all run out of ideas to torture us?" I tease, reaching out and poking Aidan in the ribs. He flinches in surprise, and raises a finger in warning. But the smile never leaves, always there to greet me with its charm.

"It's our favorite sport, actually," he retorts, taking my hand to walk side by side.

"You have to admit, that test was borderline excessive." If it's easy for me to understand how the first challenge in Greensburg, and the chase in Ursley, are useful to determine if we would be a good choice for the team, the one they put us through tonight feels unnecessary.

Since Marcus got detained and transferred until his trial, Luca, Rafael, and I had to undergo a slightly different scenario this time. Earlier tonight, War and the circle had us collaborate as partners to simulate a heist. My first thought was why War would need us to simulate robbing a bank, but when they gave us the plan, I realized it was more complex. What we were supposed to rob was a truckload of weapons—a convoy full of assault weapons in transit, no less.

"We needed to see how you'd work with people you hated," Aidan answers.

Slowing down since we reached our destination, I fully turn to face him. "I don't *hate* them. We're competing against each other. It's different. Hate has nothing to do with that," I declare.

Aidan puts his backpack on the tall grass and crouches down to get the blanket out of it. While shaking the material to flatten it on the ground, he says, "Okay, so if I told you the favorite so far was Rafael, how'd that make you feel?" he says jokingly.

Rolling my eyes, I position myself in front of him to help smooth it down. Once we do, I kneel on the edge and trap my hands between my legs to avoid showing him how my body betrays my feelings about our very first date.

"For one, I wouldn't trust you. Maybe the third test was a complete failure because all of us wanted to be the leader, but I nailed the first and the second. By a *mile*." I emphasize with a nod, knowing I finished in the first position on both challenges. Aidan revealed to me War was impressed. As if he didn't think I was capable of it, despite the months of completing his jobs without problems. It's far easier to judge my accomplishments when I'm alone at night rather than in the middle of the action. Alone, I even dare congratulate myself. When the crippling doubts assail me, it's a lot harder to have rational thoughts.

Aidan settles on the blanket in front of me, extending his legs on either side of my body and maintaining his upper body upright with his arms. "That you did." His knowing smile gives me enough confidence for whatever they're planning next. Despite the secrets he initially kept from me, the more I get to know him, the more I realize he's an open book to me. "But failing the third, like you said, doesn't look good for *any* of you."

I straighten up on my knees and drop forward. On all fours right in front of his face, I grin and peck him, snatching his bag from beside him. Sitting back on my folded legs, I open the backpack and get the snacks out. The efforts drained me, my stomach grumbles with hunger.

"Why is that? It's not like all of us will work for War. Chances are, we're not going to see each other at all after the new member is decided," I point out, a mouthful of baby carrots he packed for us, my favorite.

He laughs, though I'm not sure why. "Working as a team is as important as working solo. If you can't manage to put aside your bitterness—or opinions—how will you do among us?"

His kind smile not disappearing, I run my tongue over my lips to check if I have a piece there. It prompts him to reach for my arm, holding the bag of vegetables and dragging me to his body. I gasp, surprised, and almost fall on him. But at the last second, Aidan catches me by the waist and guides me so my back rests securely on his front. Dropping a kiss on my hair, I unfold my legs and extend them similarly to his.

"It's not the same," I complain, munching loudly.

"It is. At first, we're all strangers knowing everyone's secrets, but with time, everything changes. We're a family," he whispers into my ear, extending his fingers to show me the tattoos on his knuckles.

A *family*—a word that barely means anything to me anymore. Not even the blood ties can bring loyalty. How can I trust those I work with?

"Would you call someone your family if they've done something you despise?" I murmur, caressing his fingers, then flattening his hand on my stomach. My eyes lift to the unobstructed night sky, where stars glow. I don't know this place—this calm piece of heaven on a hill, overlooking the city of Ursley. From here, we can see everything. The cars are as small as little toys and the city lights, tiny spots compared to the ones on top of our heads. A relaxing environment I needed after the stress of tonight's mission.

"We've all done something we aren't proud of. War first. Everyone has regrets, dreams, and plans to change. That's what brings us together—walking in the same direction while learning how to heal from our past." His voice is like a melody, a gentle caress over my skin.

I inhale, trying to form a coherent sentence in my mind before telling him everything. But before I can utter a word, Aidan interrupts me.

Raising his hand once again in front of our faces, he clenches his fist and lifts only one finger—his index—on which the letter '*B*' is adorned with a beautiful cloud and shattered glass around it. "I told you most of my tattoos mean a friend of mine who is dead or in prison. Six years ago, Benjamin and I were helping another friend with a job, but it ended badly. The police got involved, and it was all my fault because I was the one who had to make sure the security system was properly turned off. My mistake forced Ben to kill a cop to protect me, but he didn't see the one behind him with his gun pointed at his head. I got away, but he died," he reveals lowly, still tortured by the memory.

Putting my snacks on the blanket, I silently curl against his torso.

He raises a second finger, this time, the thumb from his other hand. The letter '*R*' is written in a gothic font, a single rose contorting around it. "Rose was my first girlfriend. We met because, for financial reasons, boys and girls shared the same classes. Yes, in juvie, I know how *romantic*," he chuckles, and I match the expression. "She had a thing with ravens. Always trying to convince me they were some sort of spies from the government. She also had a heroin addiction."

"Oh my god," I whisper, fearing what comes next.

"No, no, she's alive. At least, she was the last time I've heard about her. Going to rehab was one thing she had to do if she wanted to be free," he explains. His tattooed hand comes to the side of my face and brushes the hair flying behind my ear. "She had to be clean for five months prior to release, but I discovered one night she paid a girl to switch their urine sample. I knew from seeing around me what drugs could do to someone. It was terrifying seeing all those people lose themselves completely until the next fix was the only thing keeping them going."

He exhales heavily, dropping his hand and lowering his chin to rest on my head. "Even though we were kids, I knew she'd never forgive me for snitching on her, yet I did it anyway. She eventually ended up in prison when she was caught dealing. This time she was an adult, so no second chances," he ends.

"Would you have done something different if you could go back in time?" I ask, my mind bursting with thoughts of my own story and the multiple decisions I could've avoided if I stopped once to think.

"No. But I would've tried helping her instead of pointing at her problems," he reveals. I had my doubts long before Aidan confessed about his past, long before tonight. War trusts his circle because, like he said, they're the only people who have lost enough to go past their individual troubles in the name of this family. A family with a heavy past, yet one willing to turn a blind eye to their mistakes if they prove they can change and still grow.

The boss is a man who survives in this jungle because he knows how to leverage his knowledge. He removed himself from the feud in Greensburg to build something he knew was worth it. Worth fleeing everything he had always known for something yet to be built. Because *he* changed, but those people over there never did. They evolved into *monsters* and power-hungry *beasts*. Those mob clans never regret and would go to great lengths to assert their dominance. Not War. Not Aidan. They would rather use what they've done, accept those regrets, and do better. Not in terms of doing something good, but to consider the consequences and problems every action could cause.

I understand now—clearly. The tests are not only meant to challenge our skills and decision-making process, but to show we can learn from our faults.

Slowly, I straighten and pull away myself from him. A deep frown contorts my features when I look at him. "You know," I speak these words in the dead of the night, putting an end to these months of doubts and worries. Thinking Aidan would never let me get close to him if he knew, yet all this time, he held this information. He was testing me from the beginning.

"Are you mad at me?" With a fleeting glance, he repeats the same question I'd asked him a few days earlier.

Unlike him, I don't hide the truth. My shoulders shrug as I, too, avoid his stare. "Offended you haven't told me. Relieved, also."

He emits a non-committal sound as he nods. "I'm sorry. I wanted to give you time to tell me. When I considered you for the spot, War gave me your file. He said I must study who you are before trusting you with something like that," he reveals, shame coating his words.

"Was everything just an elaborate plan?" I rasp, not containing the hurtful feeling transpiring from my heart. "Was every interaction we had just a *test*?"

Aidan quickly adjusts his posture and hardens his stare. "Absolutely *not*, Jade," he vows convincingly.

"Work has nothing to do with what happens between you and me."

I get up to walk away, giving myself room to breathe and think clearly. Obviously, he follows. "Aidan, it's a *lot* to take in," I complain, feeling overwhelmed and unsure of what to trust. I want to believe him, and I want to *build* something with him. But I can't shake off the feeling I'm just a pawn. I'm convinced I am.

"I know, I'm *sorry*. You have every right to walk away from it all."

"*Walk away?*" I repeat, confused why he mixes everything up. "I won't walk away. I've done too much for War, I'm in this until the end. It's just hard to believe you're choosing me despite what you've read about me. And *why* the hell you keep all those secrets from me."

Closing the distance between us, Aidan reaches for my waist and I let him. "We've been betrayed in the past. Not by one, but by *many* people. Some we trusted decided to run back to Greensburg with valuable information about War. I don't want to say we were doubting you because, truthfully, I never did. Like I told you, the boss has a hard time putting his trust in someone new. I'm so sorry it hurt you, especially when you thought all this time I would somehow push you away once I learned about your past. But you *have* to see it our way. It was a hard decision, still is. But you've done enough to show us where you stand," he admits, tortured by the lie. Because it's what he did.

"You said no more lies, no more secrets," I remind him, my voice cracking.

"Yet, I've kept this from you," he breathes out, admitting his fault. "I'm sorry, Jade. I read your file, I know about your past. We tested you without your knowledge *or* consent. I apologize for our methods. I truly *am* sorry."

I exhale, knowing it's pointless to argue, because I understand why he did it. It doesn't make it okay, but I think I would've done the same, too. "Is there anything else?" I ask softly, looking at our feet.

His index finger comes to my chin to raise my head high. The determination in his gaze is familiar, which has some effect on my body. "*No.* It's the entire truth this time. It's *everything*. But if you doubt me, ask questions, and I'll answer them truthfully. Call War, and he'll tell you the same." Slightly bending over, his palm comes warming my cheek while his lips brush the other in a delicate kiss. "I haven't forgotten about what you said," he whispers.

The fog obstructing my brain has me shaking my head to dissipate it. He is intoxicating, my judgment turns weaker when he's around. "What did I say?"

A smirk forms on his expression. Kissing my nose, he then bites his lips before explaining himself. "I think I might have a spot on my neck," he declares, raising a finger to brush the skin of his nape, showing me the small patch of untouched skin between the ink here and there. "For the tattoo you'll have me do."

I puff out some air, amused. Rolling my eyes, yet finding it endearing he wants to hold the promise. After all, it wasn't much of a sacrifice, and seeing his body, I can only be sure of one thing with Aidan—he will always fulfill a promise.

I hum. "A snake," I announce smugly. "That's what we call someone who is deceiving. A backstabber, right?" I mock, playing with him.

He hisses. "I deserve it." The grin finally finds its rightful place on his face, brightening the night once again when I lift on my toes to kiss him.

"So, that *date*, Aidan. I think we nailed the *'getting to know each other better'* part, don't you think?" I playfully say, snatching his hand in mine to drag him back to the blanket.

Behind me, he giggles in good humor. "Yeah, totally. My girl thinks I'm a backstabber. I'm going to marry her," he jokes.

I snort, glancing over my shoulder at his blissful expression. "Would you let your girl stay at your place for a few days?" I tempt, hopeful.

On our spot under the stars, he falls ungracefully to the ground, pulling on my arm so I land on him, too. "You can stay as long as you want. Why? Is there a problem?" he inquires, as he strokes my hair back with me sitting astride him.

"I'm not sure. No one can enter Greensburg at the moment. There's been an explosion. They say it comes from underground—*Oh.*" As dots connect themselves in my head, my expression morphs into astonishment. "War *did it?*" I burst out. The map he had us retrieve had a purpose. This test wasn't one—it was a job in disguise.

"No. It wasn't us. He sold the info to a powerful family there," he replies.

Every action has a consequence. It's the snowball effect—If I hadn't met War, I would've never raced on The Serpent Circuit, never been dragged into this competition, never stolen this map. War would've never sold it. The warehouse in Greensburg and the forced quarantine would've never happened. The smallest, seemingly insignificant impact I have on the world could turn into a disaster. How can I not feel responsible for everything happening everywhere?

"Jade." Aidan cups my face. "Get out of your head," he whispers softly.

My features relax ever so slightly. I let myself be overwhelmed by the look in his eyes, the shadow of his eyelashes on his irises, his parted lips, and his warm palms over my cheeks. I blink and pinch my lips to contain the adoring look I must have. The utter devotion born not so long ago.

"Maybe it's best if I stay. You'll help me focus." I glance around us when his hands leave my face, smiling to myself for what I'm about to say. "Maybe you could train me for the other test that'll surely come, right?" I pry, unsubtly.

Aidan shakes his head, but I see it in his eyes: he wants to tell me something. "You shouldn't do this," he resists. "I can't tell you yet."

"Tell me what?"

He drops his head back, and I watch as he groans to the sky. "I can't."

"Oh, come *on*. Just this once," I try, caressing his charcoal hair shining when the wind makes the strands dance. I get closer and kiss his jaw, which has him lowering his head to watch me.

"There are no more tests," he caves immediately.

That was easy.

"No more? So, you made your decision?" I push further, malice and contempt all over my face. He tries to resist again, clenching his jaw and pinching his lips. But I tilt my head to the side and give him heart-eyes, hoping it's enough to make him spill what he knows.

"You already know who I'll vote for," he hints with a wink, making it even more obvious by never averting his gaze from mine. Once again, I'm reminded Aidan has to be the most attractive person I know.

"My number one fan," I tease, taking his bag and getting our dinner out with an easy and unbothered smile. Spending the night in his company turns out to be my new favorite hobby. And I know for sure that from now on, it's no longer a dream and there will be no more *'what-ifs.'*

the bird is finally free

CHAPTER 14
In Ursley.

This feeling of believing myself indestructible once the sun goes down affects Aidan. We have spent hours on this blanket, talking about our dreams and goals. Making reckless plans to travel the world and drive aimlessly for days on end.

Laughing at the jokes he makes, kissing passionately, and getting lost in his voice as he tells funny stories from his childhood. He wants to know everything about me, every emotion. We've spent those hours looking into each other's eyes, memorizing our features and tracing them with our fingers. Progressively and without warning me, I've grown attached to him to the point of knowing I'm incapable of letting him go. This moment was meant to happen between us. He cracks my shell open and extends his arm to help me get out, until I can fully stand on my own. Aidan remains on my side, showing me his support yet letting me decide for my future.

"The sun is going up," he whispers, saddened, laid down by my side, like I am.

With the dark leaving us, the perfect feeling evaporates like a mist blown out. I never want to let go—I want this moment to last a little longer. "One of these nights, when the vote happens, and the circle has taken its decision, we should take our cars and drive around Ursley," I share my wish, a tender smile on my lips. Watching like he does the horizon getting lighter by the second.

Aidan turns his head to look at me, a twinkle in his eyes. "You want to race me?" he suggests mischievously.

"*Well*, I was thinking about a simple ride. Are you sure you want to find out which is better?" I pivot on my side, tucking both my hands under my head to serve as a pillow and fold my legs.

Staying on his back, he lifts his arms and traps them under his head. He hums, contemplating if his self-assurance is tricking his judgment or not. "That could be fun. But on one condition." He removes one arm from under his head to raise a finger in the air while looking up.

I giggle as I shift my body closer to his, resting my knees over his hip. "Which is?" I murmur close to his ear. My breath, as well as the warmth of my body glued to his, makes his limbs slightly tremble. It would be impossible not to notice the goosebumps erupting all over his exposed arms.

When he turns his head in my direction, I get closer again, making our noses graze softly. I rest my head on his biceps and cover his chest with my arm.

"You'll drive the Mazda and I, the Nissan," he mouths silently. Only the sound of his lips forming the words reaches my ear.

The corners of my mouth curl up. "Are you scared I may be better? That's why you want to put me in a car I've never driven before?" I tease, raising my chin to stroke the tip of his nose with mine.

He puffs on my face amusingly, making my hair fly over my shoulder. "Not a chance. I'm doing this for *you.*"

Feeling the competitiveness awakening once again, I turn my eyes into slits. "Oh, Aidan. You have no idea what you've started," I threaten challengingly.

I expect a direct friendly confrontation, a call for adrenaline again, yet I'm solely mistaken when, in the next instant, as soon as the comment left my mouth, Aidan reacts in a flash. He jumps on my body and traps my head between his palms to crash his lips into mine. My legs open on themselves, pressing his pelvis onto mine with my calves pushing on his thighs.

He devours me with an intensity I've come to love from him, taking the lead and moving my jaw as he wants it. Aidan breathes my air selfishly, leaving me with little, forcing my brain to only be satisfied with this passion. I whimper, the desire awakened and the pulsation between my legs growing insistent.

Everything is swift, immediate, like muscle memory or singing along with a song I've known my whole life. It's what the present feels like with him: familiar yet exciting. It never gets old, it's always comforting and exhilarating.

Suddenly, he refuses me his lips, moving his head away in urgency. "Have you—what we've talked about?" he lets out confusingly, not sure he's making any sense with the arousal already obstructing his focus.

Yet I understand him perfectly. I nod multiple times, humming and forcing him to kiss me again. But as always, he needs my vocal confirmation, which I'll never grow tired of. How perfect he is. "Yes, I'm on birth control now." I chose him, as he did me. It's only natural we talked about it, agreed to test ourselves and take this step. I only want him, without barriers, without space—as ridiculous as the space might be.

He shakes his head once. It's all he needed to continue. His hands slowly descend along my neck, my shoulders. When I feel his palms kneading my breasts, I push my chest forward, wanting more of him. As if the current moment isn't enough. I wish I'd have him under my skin.

I grip his hair, tear on it to get myself some air. Apparently, the eagerness with which I needed to inhale the life back into my lungs is funny to him. My throat lets out a groan I can't control. And when I push on my elbows to lift myself up, I capture the skin of his neck between my lips. Sucking and nibbling the flesh there, right on the spot he showed me the tattoo would soon come.

His moaning sends vibrations I can feel on the tip of my nose. Panting, he wraps an arm around my lifted upper body to maintain my position as he plants his knees onto the blanket and begins to make rocking movements with his hips, giving the both of us the necessary friction to ignite our bodies a little more. Our jeans, the perfect ally to his actions.

I drop my head back and sob loudly when my heart skips some beats. Aidan gently lays me back down and sits on his haunches between my parted legs. Without leaving my gaze, he snatches the hem of his shirt and throws it over his head. As quickly, he opens his jeans and drags the zipper down. He lunges forward, but catches himself with his hands positioned on either side of my chest.

I do my best to control my erratic heartbeat, but one look in his dark, hooded eyes, and I'm coming undone. "Touch me," I plead. "*Aidan*," I beg shamelessly.

Taking his tongue out to moisten his lips, he slowly lowers his body back on mine and grinds hardly over my clothed clit. The sensations he provokes have the effect of a thousand electric shocks right into my brain. Sending me signals to tear my clothes off and spread my legs as wide as I can.

His full lips find mine again as I lower my hands between us to unfasten my jeans. His tongue makes gentle circles around mine, progressively slowing down to savor the moment instead of surrendering to our most primal instinct.

Feeling the struggle of lowering my jeans, he takes over the task and grips both my pants and underwear in the process. I wiggle my hips, never wanting to leave the delicious taste of his lips, which makes him laugh. "Baby, I've got you," he reassures me. In the blink of an eye, he lifts my legs and drags the clothes off, tossing them beside us on the blanket. When my feet touch the ground, I spread my knees and expose myself to him, feeling the fresh yet comfortable air tingle my core, already dripping wet for him. "I have to warn you, this place is a lot more popular than the bridge," he confesses, amused, probably because he's well on his way to making me orgasm in every corner of this city.

I inhale slowly as he waits for my decision. But a smirk finds its way to my lips, and I raise a suggestive eyebrow. "Well, we better hurry then," I reply playfully.

Not wasting any more time, Aidan lowers his jeans and underwear to his mid-thighs, uncovering his erection now bobbing in the air. Trying something different, he clutches my ankles in his fists and lifts them over his head, bending my body in half. Adjusting our position, he then gathers my legs on one side, allowing me to rest my calves over one of his shoulders.

Utterly at his mercy, unable to move a muscle right now, I realize my body compressing over my lower belly will undoubtedly heighten the sensations. A thought immediately answered when he sinks deep inside me. Groaning at feeling us joined in the most intimate ways, Aidan can't help himself but watch with unshaking attention the way his cock penetrates me, and produces the squelching sounds surrounding us with his constant actions.

Hypnotized by him, I forget about the whistles of the wind, the gentle air messing with his hair, or the sun now timidly warming our skin. This connection we share is enough to shut the world out and create our own.

Aidan transfers his weight from both legs to one and shifts his body so his cock strokes me enticingly. My head spins with pleasure, and it doesn't take me long before I embrace the moment and let my worries fade away. His in-and-out movements grow impossibly fast, almost putting his full weight on my bent legs. He prevents me from wiggling too much and keeps going to give us better momentum to have him dive inside of me.

"Don't stop, baby please. I love it. I love it, Aidan. Please, don't stop, I'm almost there," I chant. The sounds coming out of his mouth are uncontrollable, betraying his chase to finish as fast as he can. We're reckless and stupid. But we're young, and that's what is beautiful. Someone might come, yet nothing matters. Not when he's in my arms and he watches me like I hold all the answers in my eyes.

Plunging one last time to the hilt, he drops his head against my chest and remains motionless as the power of his orgasm swipes his consciousness altogether. When he opens his eyes on me, he must see my desperation. Immediately, he responds to my silent plea by kissing me passionately. After biting my lips, he resumes his thrusting even though I can already feel his cock softening. Against his lips, I open my mouth and shout out, "Aidan, Aidan, don't stop! I'm coming," I urge him, my tone pressing and frantic.

Focusing on my orgasm, I tense my muscles and lock my lungs. He stops kissing me to better observe the moment I'll let go for him. When I do, it's in an explosion that shatters me from the inside out, as I gasp and thrash with the power of my release. He continues to rock his hips until the last of it washes over me.

My senses come back one by one, and I take my time to brush my lips over his—not kissing, just touching lightly and smiling. As we enjoy the calm, he lowers my legs as slowly as he can—inch by inch—while I'm hissing and gritting my teeth the whole time.

"I'm sorry," he apologizes, yet only showing me his white teeth, grinning like an idiot.

"Maybe—maybe we should invest in an inflatable mattress to keep in the car. This can't continue like this," I advise, but he doesn't take me seriously. Instead of agreeing, he bursts out laughing, still covering me with his naked body.

"We should," he agrees, his words saying one thing and his face saying another.

My eyes close when he supports his upper body on his elbows and brushes my hair back, expertly massaging my skull. "I don't think you're my friend, Aidan. I don't think that's only what we are. I want you forever," I announce, leaving half of my brain—and reason—out the window because the morning sun is stunning, his breath strokes my skin, and his heat makes my heart flutter.

For a split-second, he halts his movements. "Then I'll be with you forever," he promises, tracing the length of my nose with the tip of his.

Not far from us, a curious noise reaches my ears, but I have trouble recognizing it. Because I'm too engrossed in the happy humming the naked man is making on me.

"*Oh, fu*—Jade, baby, get up." Aidan's panic has me instantly on high alert. My hearing is suddenly hijacked by the barking of a dog approaching at a terrifying speed. In a flash, Aidan stands above me, his pants already fastened, rushing my legs into my underwear. Successive actions have my brain lagging slightly. But I pull myself together and, in no time, it's no longer exhibitionism we could be accused of, but public indecency. Still just as bad, I admit, but less serious according to the law.

In fact, he and I choose the hasty decision: seeing a dog and its owners jogging toward us, we abandon the idea of dressing up. Instead, we pick up our things and *run*. Aidan—shirtless—and I—without my jeans—are caught up in hysterical laughter as we sprint as fast as we can to the car.

Unlocking it, I jump on the left side of his RX-7 and throw the blanket under my bottom to sit on it. I wiggle as best as I can to put my pants on when he appears on my side fully clothed. He slams the door behind him, his laughter still going strong.

"When I took you here for our date, I didn't plan for us to have sex, you know," he points out, somehow putting the whole event on *me*.

I gape at him, challenging him to tell the truth, but he remains unfazed. "You're lying. You know we always end up having sex when we're outside because you love it," I remind him matter-of-factly. It's one reason we're so compatible.

"Say the rest, Jade," he pressures, amusingly.

"I don't know what you're talking about." I pretend to ignore him, but my façade crumbles when he starts tickling me again. A godawful sound escapes my sealed lips, but I refuse to admit anything to his face.

"*Jade*," he warns, pinching my side, until I can't take it anymore and beg him to stop. "*Say the rest.*"

I scream again, but he ignores me once more. "Okay, okay," I finally surrender. "*We* do, alright." His hands don't leave me, but he finally stops teasing my sensitive areas. I'm left in an awkward, half-bent position, with my legs curved on themselves on the seat. My back to his, he cuddles me with an arm and squeezes me against him. With half my body resting against his, he kisses my hair and waits for me to recover. A breathless chuckle escapes me when I realize how good it feels to have a friend. Because whatever happens in our relationship, we'll always support each other. "I mean it. I really want you with me forever," I whisper, noticing the atmosphere slightly changing. "I don't care if I join War's drivers circle, I just want to be with you."

"Even if I hurt you when I lied?" he asks, his tone letting me easily guess he has remorse about it.

With his arms securely wrapped around me, I couldn't feel better, more at *home*, finally. "When I was in college and the,"—I gulp loudly—"accident happened, everything I ever was suddenly vanished. I made a mistake, and it's entirely my fault she died. But it *hurt* when my friends stopped talking to me, when my parents acted like I didn't exist anymore. I wanted to do better. I was willing to work on myself and learn from that tragedy to do good instead. They showed me they didn't care because I was now the one who ended a life, and that's the kind of mistake that's forever ingrained into someone's being. They made me understand no matter how much progress I made, I would never deserve anyone's forgiveness," I speak softly.

Sharing my experience with Aidan feels right. I'm not looking for answers from him, yet voicing them to him feels like easing all my pain.

"If they don't want to see you change, to see you've grown, it's their loss. And if they couldn't see how much it hurt you, how you reached out but they turned away, screw them. You're allowed to grieve, to feel sorry, and to seek forgiveness." His words, filled with conviction and power, deeply affect me. My throat constricts and my chin wobbles. So, I let go and slouch and squeeze myself against him as the tears run down my face.

"Thank you," I breathe out, too low for my voice to carry. But he heard me. He heard me, so he holds me tighter, kisses my head, draws closer, and brushes his lips against my cheek while using his thumb to wipe away my tears.

"It's okay, Jade. It's all going to be okay," he promises, murmuring while stroking my hair with affection.

Feeling the need to change the subject to gather my strength back again, I rest his arm under my breasts and play with his fingers. The story of that '*B*' comes to mind, and I trace the back of his hand, the tattoo of a caged bird with broken wings. "Tell me about this one," I mumble timidly. "Please."

Aidan, having closed his eyes and rested his forehead against the crown of my head, takes a look at the tattoo before resuming his position. "It's the first tattoo I had made once I got out of prison. I was eighteen and feeling *poetic*." He lets out a breathy chuckle at his younger self. It's true it's pretty easy to understand the meaning of it—the lack of freedom, the discipline, and threatening environment.

"I think it's beautiful." When I close my eyes, I can picture the details of many of his tattoos already. Some on his torso, the words on his lids, the initials. I can see their shapes and hidden secrets without a single doubt.

That realization brings a smile to my face.

the rest of my life

CHAPTER 15

War's garage in Ursley.

Unlike what I was led to believe, doing business in daylight isn't much of a problem when your name is War. After isolating his inner circle—his drivers, spies, and other allies—to vote for which candidate will have the privilege to join them, a decision has been made. Midday has come, and I've never felt so impatient to know about my future.

Today is Sunday, the only day of the week none of his regular employees are present on site.

"I can't," Luca announces, raising his hands in surrender. "I can't take it. Going out for a smoke." He, Rafael, and I can't sit still for long in the customer waiting room of the garage as the simple thought of having to count each second passing drives us mad. I understand the reaction and the need to occupy my mind with anything rather than the agonizing wait.

With hurried steps, Luca exits through the glass door and paces in front of it, lighting his cigarette at the same time. While I try my best to calm my tense muscles, I can't seem to control the fidgeting of my leg. I look as Rafael has decided to take his phone out to play a game. A minute ago, he was sipping coffee. Before that, he was taking a quiz in the magazines, and then scraping the dirt out of his soles with a pen lying around.

Dropping my head back against the wall, I let my thoughts wander for a minute. How is it that I find myself waiting in this room? How is it that I feel no pressure to hide from people, from my life in Greensburg since I met everyone here? The answer is rather simple: I've changed. It took time, but Aidan was right—I changed. My motivations have shifted long before I agreed to partake in this competition. If I'm honest with myself, I'd say I knew I'd agree to anything War would've asked of me at any point. When money isn't a problem anymore, my real self comes through. I like the chase, the races, and the beating of my heart when it's so fast it's painful. I've always liked the sensation, but didn't believe I could do it on my own. Aidan's schemes had me realize I like it. Screw going down the wrong path and choosing to spend the rest of my life in the gray territory. The underground world is *perfect* for me.

At the sound of steps approaching, Rafael and I react promptly, straightening up and focusing on the manager's office door—Aidan's office. When he appears with a serious expression on his face, not letting anything transpire, Luca hurries back inside. "You can come in," Aidan announces, turning around and going back in, expecting us to follow.

For a brief moment, the guys and I look at each other in confusion. We've all been in his office before. There's no way War's entire team is inside. Deciding not to question it further, Rafael shrugs and takes the lead. It's when we enter after him we realize the imposing shelf at the back serves as a decoy for a passage to the basement.

In line, we silently go down the stairs until we find ourselves in a large room lit by neon lights on the ceiling. In the middle is a table where we meet War and his men. The absence of women had never struck me as much as it did today. I have no reason to feel uncomfortable, but the curious eyes of all these people I've never met before make me uneasy and slightly self-conscious.

As if by instinct, my eyes search for Aidan. Finding him watching me as he takes his place alongside the other drivers I've met, I calm my nerves when I notice the reassuring twitch on his face. A sign he wishes to smile at me, yet has to hide it for the time being.

We stand tall in front of the table, in a line for everyone to examine us. While Rafael and Luca on each side of me effortlessly remain still, I have to strain myself to do the same.

"You must know it wasn't easy to make a decision. You have all proven yourself capable and motivated," War's gruff voice resonates all around the room. "For the sake of *democracy*," he amusedly lets out, "everyone in this room had to vote. Because it's not a new driver we welcome, but an addition to our family."

My eyes wander around, looking into the many emotionless faces. Some men have many tattoos, like Aidan, but they look terrifying in comparison. Some have scars, others do not. Some are dressed casually when others are in more formal attire. I think it's the overall diverse family that has me on the edge of my seat.

"The current drivers and I have chosen candidates according to personal criteria, but the others only based their decisions on your performances. The results of the many challenges we put you through," the boss adds.

My shoulders sag an inch and the sudden intake of breath has been noticed by my boyfriend who hasn't stopped watching me. He has to actively clear his throat and lean on the table to hide the now evident smile behind his hands. This obvious reaction gives me all I need to know.

I completed both solo tests, but not the last one. I raced alongside supercars in Frost on a demanding half-dirt circuit and finished second. I've worked for War for many months and always achieved what he expected of me. I was born in Greensburg and know these streets as if their layout were imprinted in my memory.

It's a given.

"Jade, congratulations," War announces proudly, a rare friendly smile spreading from ear to ear on his features. I'm part of War and Aidan's family now. I'm no longer on my own.

I'm not alone anymore.

My immediate response is to contain my happiness in the face of the other two candidates in respect. But as someone gets up and takes them out of the room, I let myself show how much this means to me.

The first to come meet me is the boss himself, patting my shoulders in support and squeezing them without a word. He's not going to say he's sorry he doubted me or he wanted to get rid of me. He won't apologize because why would he? It might be a family, yet he's still the boss. I don't feel the need to remind him, either. If anything, this might be the reason my competitiveness grew unstoppable. It fueled my fire and motivated me. Maybe it was his plan from the beginning. However, War is and will remain a terrifying man to me. It's no wonder I pinch my lips painfully as to not appear weak in front of the King of the Streets.

"Thank you," I say, the words missing.

He nods in acknowledgment, right before we're interrupted by his phone. When he fishes the device out of his pocket and looks at the caller, his behavior changes ever so slightly. Straightening just a fraction, his frown deepening, betraying his surprise.

"Miss me?" he answers the call, turning away from me. My stare is captured by his imposing figure as he goes up the stairs.

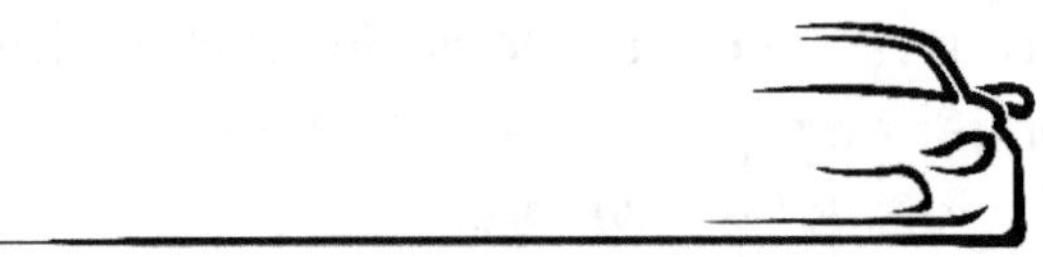

"This is slightly overwhelming," I utter softly, letting my senses relax with the fresh bottle of soda between my hands. Sitting on a workbench, I watch distractedly as a shirtless Aidan works on an Evo X, the temperature rising several degrees. The neon lights emphasize the sweat on his back, making his muscles shine alluringly. The tattoos twist with each of his movements, and I'm hypnotized by it.

Peering at me from under the hood, he wipes his brows with his forearm and sends a smirk my way, as if he knows exactly what I'm doing. "You'll get used to it. At first, it's going to be hard to be accepted by them all, but it'll come fast. Try not to worry about it, alright?"

Hours have passed since War's announcement of including me in the inner circle. While everyone seemed welcoming, accepting their congratulations makes me feel like a *fraud*. I'm confident in my skills, but why do my achievements make me a better choice than Luca or Rafael? Even Marcus was the best among us. He controlled his cars and emotions like he was already a part of this family.

"I'll try," I breathe out, not really believing it.

Aidan puffs and resumes his tasks.

Everyone is currently in some kind of transition. Earlier, when War received a call, he abruptly left. Something changed in the people he watches in Greensburg. The unstable relations between the mafia organizations are taking my city by storm. A big threat is looming over everyone's head. The men speak in hushed tones, but the names Madd Ryder, the Council, and Luxuria come up more than once. I overheard Apocalys being mentioned, too.

"*Jade,*" Aidan demands my attention, as he would with a child looking for trouble. A muscle in his back twitches when he dismantles a component in the engine block.

"Uh-huh?" I hum in recognition, knowing I shouldn't lose myself in my head.

"Did you, or did you not, ask me to teach you how to properly install a turbocharger?" Aidan asks teasingly, briefly glancing at me.

I bite my lips to hide the smile. "I did," I admit, jumping off the workbench and slowly approaching his back. An inch behind him, bent over, I trace his spine with the tip of my middle finger.

"If you distract me, the car will not be ready for tomorrow, and my customer will be pissed," he warns, lacking the needed threatening tone that would make me behave.

"Speaking of." Kissing with affection his bare shoulder, then straightening up to cross my arms over my chest, I wonder, "Everyone has some kind of occupation outside doing things for War. What should I do? I'm not a mechanic, I have no degrees, and I need a job I can leave as soon as you call," I complain. As they all explained to me, my priority should be War now. I can forget about driving around. I'm already having a hard time coming to terms with the fact I might have to move to Ursley permanently.

Abandoning the task of tightening bolts, Aidan carefully lays his tools beside him and turns to face me. "You can do whatever you want. If you want to stay here, we could use someone working in the garage. Not as a mechanic, but taking my place in the office: calling the customers and stuff I can't do when I'm working here. Or you can go back to Greensburg and continue driving. The missions don't happen on a whim. You'll have time to get back here," he affirms. I'd thank him for everything he's done for me, but the sweat beads on his forehead, the damp hair making him look like a model, have my brain short-circuiting.

"I'll think about it," I utter, shutting the world around off and taking the last step, separating us to jump into his arms. Laughing at my sudden change, he catches me nonetheless. Crashing my body to his, securing my frame in his arms and dropping my bottom on the car's open hood behind.

I kiss him with abandon because there's nothing that can possibly take us away from each other. Arching my back to press my supple breasts against his fiery skin makes me shake with eagerness.

"Did you turn off the cameras?" I whisper before darting my tongue out to taste the dampness running down his neck. Aidan groans loudly, dropping his head back and squeezing my bottom firmly.

"From the moment I knew it'd be only you and me," he reveals. His grip doesn't lessen, not even when he crashes my hips to his. The part of my stomach showing between my low-rise jeans and my top brushes his lower belly, which is all it takes before I grab his nape and pull his face to mine. go past that point of consciousness and become a wreaking mess too quickly.

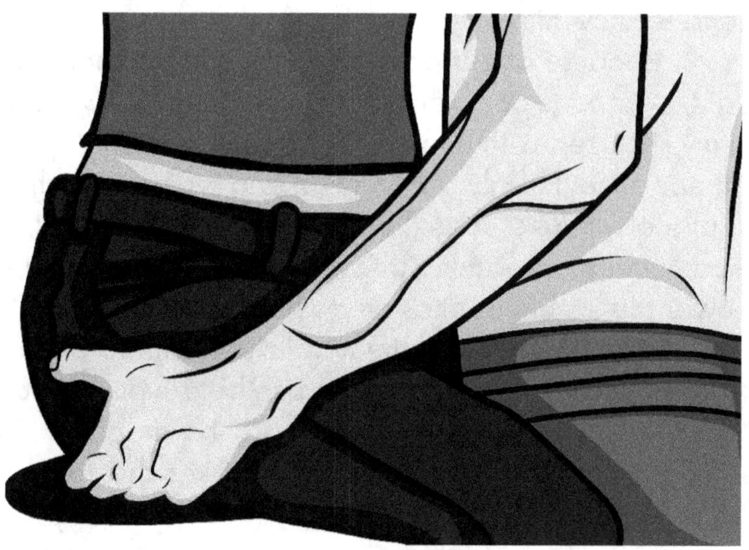

My mouth dances with his, explores with his. The utter silence of the garage is broken by our explicit whimpering. His hands roam the expanse of my back under my shirt while I can't help teasing his nipples—pulling and scratching at them does strange things to my body.

He curses, a pained expression etched on his brows. "I need to be inside you, Jade." Without wasting any more time, my fingers fumble with my jeans. I jump off the hood to lower them and my panties completely. My heart has started a frantic rhythm, betraying my impatience for his cock. My pussy tingles with desire, and I have to stroke myself to ease the ache.

Aidan traps his jeans below his bottom, lifts me onto the hood again, and hooks my knees on his elbows. Open and ready, I beg for him to fill me. "Baby please, hurry. I'm ready," I pant, spreading my inner lips with a hand to show him just as much.

Because of our position, forcing him to hold me tight, I grab his penis and run it along my slit. Coated in my slick, red with engorged blood, I point the tip at my entrance. Merely guiding him and maintaining him in place while he does the pushing in. "*Oh*, my god," I moan sweetly, breathing through gritted teeth from the power this simple act has on my heart rate.

My man thrusts all the way in, drops his forehead to mine, and lets me adjust to his size before pulling out. "You're so warm. Fuck, I love that," he marvels. His stroking against my soaking walls makes the tension build in my stomach, my head empties. Seeing my expression prompts him to accelerate the pace, penetrating me with greater strength. The force causes the car to rock with our passion—maybe he's also testing the suspension?

"Faster, *faster*," I plead, holding on for dear life onto his shoulders as he pounds into my cunt at an impossible speed. The groans, the whispers of encouragement aren't lost on me, and my gaze plunges into his. My eyebrows join in willingness to be good for him when he drops his forehead to mine.

"Open your mouth," he instructs almost angrily, as the effort drives him into madness. "Tongue out." I obey, tilting my head slightly back in time for my boyfriend to spit inside my mouth. I swallow, my limbs growing limp and shaking, balancing. I'm a ragdoll he uses, at his mercy, and thanking him for it. *"My girl,"* he praises, kissing my nose affectionately. A stark contrast to my vagina being deliciously abused and my bottom sore from the metal of the car.

I sob, cry out when I feel the release coming. "Faster—" My whines have Aidan's hands on my back tightening, locking me against him. I'm being lifted from the hood, but I barely register anything other than that. I think I hear tools crashing on the ground while he slams my bent body onto his length, impaling me again and again. Until I explode in a fierce fire that blazes in my womb—making me scream and suddenly still and hold air in my lungs. For just a second, while I don't breathe, stars fill my vision, my hearing shuts off.

"Jade, Jade, Jade..." Aidan chants, enjoying his much-needed orgasm right after mine. We ride high, but we do it together. I can't believe I've lived so long without him in my life.

Slowly, he rests me onto the workbench I was sitting on earlier, unwrapping my legs from his arms. I wince painfully as this has been the most straining experience we've had so far. The forest was nothing in comparison. Of course, my soreness makes him giggle. Yet, he takes the time to clean me up before mocking me—how charming.

Feeling my smile tug at my lips, I quickly grab the first tool on my left and throw it at him without much force. It falls right at his feet. "Not funny," I complain, losing the battle against my grin.

A comfortable silence settled between us, the calm of the garage returning. I haven't taken my eyes off his, fixed on his shirtless form as we regulate our breathing. Seeming to have had enough, Aidan closes the distance between us, placing himself between my parted legs. He lightly caresses my hair as I gape at this handsome man, admiring the freckles on his face. I can't help but feel a sense of belonging that I've never experienced before. The doubt about my future has vanished, replaced by the certainty of knowing I'm part of something bigger, something meaningful for me.

"What now?" I whisper, my fingers tracing the tattoos on his chest.

"Now, we build," Aidan replies, his voice filled with determination. "We build our future, together." And with that, I know that whatever lies ahead, I won't be facing it alone. With Aidan by my side and a newfound family behind me, I'm ready to take on the world.

The rest of my life starts now.

CHAPTER 16

Jade's place in Greensburg.

"I don't remember telling you the last time, but like your apartment," Aidan whispers, stroking my hair and scratching my scalp as I lie on top of him. His other hand holds the cigarette he keeps away from me. We're both naked under the covers, the moonlight casting a gentle glow in the room, and a faint breeze drifting in through the open windows. It feels like my favorite dream. My chin rests on my crossed arms over his chest, allowing me to feel his calm heartbeat beneath my fingers. From every angle, at any time, in any weather, Aidan is the most handsome man I've ever laid eyes on. He's a beautiful person who never fails to bring a naïve smile to my face with just a glimpse of his hair or tattoos.

Aidan is stunning, but seeing him at night, his sharp yet soft features illuminated by the bluish hue, is my favorite version of him. He seems like he's been crafted by the god of the night himself.

"It's just a room, nothing to be fazed by," I correct with a smile. My arm extends to run my palm over the top of his head, where a wild strand of hair falls over his forehead. Tilting my neck to the side and resting my cheek against his chest, I find myself hypnotized by the twinkle in his eyes. I'm completely under his charm, utterly hooked by who he is.

"Well, I like your room," he murmurs, puffing the white cloud out into the air, a familiar grin spreading across his face. "Have you thought about my offer?"

Exhaling gently, I bite my lip at the tempting idea, though not quite enticing enough for me. "I—" Lowering my head, I glance at the open bathroom door: the first shower I took here was a nightmare, with freezing, muddy water, and I nearly lost my life when I slipped on the broken tiles.

I wiggle my toes under the covers—it occurs to me that I didn't always have a bed. When I first rented the place, I slept on an inflatable mattress. The excuse for a kitchen behind me is where I first attempted to bake brownies, a terrible idea after a long, exhausting day. Right after I had been declined a loan I desperately needed from the bank.

This studio apartment is awful, impractical, not meant for a couple like us. But it was the first and only place that accepted me after I lost everything. After my parents told me they wished I was never born.

Raising my head again to meet his gaze, he already knows my answer, hence the gentle expression he wears. "I have thought about it," I tell him. "I'm not ready to move in with you, but maybe in a couple of months," I admit, not hiding the truth. Living with him is tempting, but working for War has been a significant change, and I need to be alone to process it all. I'm grateful for all the help they've provided. Even the boss offered to pay for a new place in Ursley and sent me a list of therapists I could see. I'm still deciding which one fits me best. But I've made a lot of progress, writing letters to my parents, telling them how I feel while respecting their boundaries and reluctance to see me again. Maybe I will apologize in person in the future, but I won't give up on them.

"Alright. We have all the time in the world," he reassures me, extending his arm to my nightstand to crush the filter on a coffee cup plate.

All the time in the world. "What time is it?" I ask, propping myself up on my forearms and scanning the room for our phones.

Reaching under the pillow, Aidan finds mine and presses the button to turn it on. "Almost four a.m. Why?"

Smiling mischievously, I rise onto my knees and lean over to press a peck to his neck, just above the snake tattoo he unwrapped yesterday morning. Then, I leave a trail of kisses along his jaw until I reach his lips. Gently brushing my mouth against his, feeling the ghost of his skin on mine, I hum. "How about a little drive? Or are you tired?" I tease, knowing this comment will wake him up.

And, as expected, Aidan swiftly wraps an arm around my waist and pulls me close. Pivoting his left leg, he turns us over, sending me against the mattress with him above me. *"A little drive?"* he asks, confused and clearly not remembering our conversation.

I reach over and smooth down the frown on his face with my thumb, raising my head to briefly peck his lips. "Uh-huh," I agree softly. "You take the 240SX, and I'll take the RX-7," I explain, watching as recollection dawns on his features.

"You want to *race* me?" he exclaims loudly, surprised and amused.

"Are you *still* scared to find out I'm better than you?"

He laughs wholeheartedly, turning his head to look out the window. Watching the empty streets, the barely visible stars, I see a softening happening in him, emotions washing over him. "You are better than me," he whispers when his gaze meets mine again.

"I'm not so sure. You're full of surprises," I comment with a slow smile, squinting my eyes with feigned annoyance.

"Let's find out then." In a flash, Aidan stands fully naked in the middle of the room, bending over to retrieve his jeans from the floor. Slowly, I unwrap the comforter from my body and search for my clothes. The childish smile never leaves either of our faces, as we both seem lost in this perfect reality. It feels like a beautiful memory, like a hot summer night, a moment I never want to end.

Drunk in passion, Aidan and I leave my apartment and race down the stairs, hand in hand. He skips a few steps, pulling me along with him. We laugh wildly, loudly, paying little attention to my sleeping neighbors or the city, which might awaken in panic at the sound of our engines roaring through the streets of Greensburg.

But it doesn't matter, because it never really did when Aidan is with me. When my friend holds my hand, my heart heals. The lump I've had in my stomach since the accident is nothing but a distant memory, because this man's smile is enough to carry me to distant lands where pain no longer exists, where forgiveness is possible.

"Are you sure you want to do this, baby?" Aidan asks over his shoulder, his expression cheerful and contagious, making me want to collapse and burst into tears, because his presence has helped me immensely. It seems insignificant, because a simple expression can't be enough to heal years of unhappiness and self-hatred, and yet with him it makes sense.

"I'm sure," I giggle like a little girl, letting go of his hand and reaching into my back pocket for the keys. Parked in front of my Nissan, his Mazda looks like a worthy challenger. His car is lighter and more sensitive, which has considerable benefits. But both vehicles are modified to the extreme, and he knows mine as well as his, having done most of the work on them.

After a quick inspection of both cars, Aidan returns to stand in front of me, his keys dangling from his index finger. "You're an amazing driver, Jade. In my eyes, you're the absolute best. But tonight, we don't take any risks, alright?" he says gently, affection visible in his eyes.

I capture his keys and his hand, bringing it to my lips. My mouth brushes over his knuckles, the many letters, the many tattoos. I dive into his gaze, feeling my throat constricting with emotion. My head shakes ever so slightly in agreement, then I lower his fist to my heart, pressing it against my chest. I know he can feel my racing heartbeat, my breathing quickening. "I promise," I mouth, erasing the distance between us, standing on my toes to kiss him tenderly. His other hand comes behind my head, his palm pressing me against his mouth a little longer.

When my eyes open again, I know with absolute clarity crossing paths with him was one of those rare events that happens only once in a lifetime. From the depths of my heart, my soul, I recognize Aidan is made for me as much as I'm made for him. I am his, will be, and always have been. His girl, his friend. "I love you," I whisper as softly as I can against his mouth, the words gently caressing his skin. A confession that will remain etched in stone.

The air coming out of his nose warms my cheeks. His thumb makes a gentle caress on my hair. "I love you too, little driver," he softly replies, raising his chin to drop a last kiss on my forehead before letting me go.

Taking his keys and giving him mine, I brush his firm stomach with my palm as I walk past him. Going around the RX-7, I unlock and open the door, glancing at him as he does the same. Grinning, I settle inside, but my attention is quickly caught by a sticky note on the steering wheel. In his handwriting, it reads, '*Did you think I'd forgotten?*'

"Of course you didn't. You always fulfill your promises," I answer aloud, smiling from ear to ear. Inserting the key and starting the car, I make the engine rev to life. Behind me, Aidan leaves the parking spot, coming to my side and looking at me through the window. He stops and turns his head to me.

Laughing, completely in love with him, I raise the note in front of the window. In response, he winks. "Are you coming?" he mouths mischievously, making the car purr to scare me, showing me he's ready for a little adrenaline.

"I'm coming," I mouth back. *I'll always follow you, Aidan. Always.*

OTHER BOOKS BY THE AUTHOR

The Apocalys Empire Series

The Apocalys Empire series is about four wealthy young women, all heiresses to massive fortunes, that decided to escape the traditional life path their parents have set for them, to create the criminal empire of their dreams.

With each installment, a *captivating new character* emerges. Capable of engaging with the reader, he will reshape the plot's trajectory for better or worse.

APOCALYS
Book One — Focused on the Quartet.

BLACKWELL BLOOD
Book One.Five — Blackwell's Family.

AN EMPIRE OF MAD(D)NESS
Book Two — Luxuria and Maddox Ryder.

AN EMPIRE OF FLAMES
Book Three — Fyra's Love Story.

AN EMPIRE OF PEACE
Book Four — Tearie's Love Story.

AN EMPIRE OF POISON
Book Five — Romana's Love Story.

Standalones

BURNOUT BABY
Jade and Aidan Love Story.

ABOUT THE AUTHOR

V, a young French woman, possesses an unbounded imagination. Her stories, which teeter between good and evil, offer violent endings, passionate romances, and surprising twists. Within her books lies a universe that will leave no reader indifferent.

CONNECT WITH ME

Newsletter: https://tinyurl.com/VRiviere-Newsletter
Twitter: @_v_riviere
Instagram: @_v_riviere
Threads: @_v_riviere
Goodreads: V. Rivière
YouTube: @v.riviere
TikTok: @vriviere
Website: vriviere.com
Email: vriviere.author@gmail.com